FATAL ENCHANTMENT

STEPHANIE DAMORE

Chapter 1

Stepping through the community center doors, I was immediately transported back in time. The large room had been transformed into a stunning ballroom reminiscent of the Regency era in England for Aunt Thelma's surprise birthday party. The walls were draped in heavy curtains of blue velvet, while an oversized chandelier cast a warm glow over the dance floor.

My eyes swept over the guests, all of whom had come dressed in their finest aristocratic attire. The women wore elegant ball gowns with flowing skirts and off-the-shoulder sleeves, while the men wore suits with tailcoats and cravats. The room was alive with the sound of soft music and the rustling of fabric as the guests twirled around the dance floor.

Thank goodness Aunt Thelma loved the gown we'd picked out for tonight. The dress was made of rich lavender silk with an empire waistline that flattered her figure. Delicate lace and a shimmering silver brooch adorned the front while the skirt fell in graceful folds to the floor and flowed gently as she walked. My aunt looked every bit like the queen she was.

"I can hardly believe my eyes. You and your friends have truly outdone yourselves," Aunt Thelma remarked as she joined me. Our surprise had gone off without a hitch. A promised night of bingo evolved into a birthday to never forget.

I smiled, feeling a sense of pride at the compliment. "We wanted to make sure your seventieth birthday was a night to remember."

"You mean my sixtieth, right dear?" Aunt Thelma replied with a mischievous smile.

"Whatever you say," I smiled warmly in return.

"What's she doing here?" Aunt Thelma's smile was quickly replaced with a frown.

"Who?" I followed Aunt Thelma's gaze, but I couldn't tell who she was referring to. It must not have been a big deal because, in the next instant, her mood shifted once more.

"Oh, there's Frederick now. Doesn't he look handsome?" Aunt Thelma's face was radiant when looking at Frederick. Her eyes were bright, and her smile wide, completely enamored as she looked upon him. I never saw her look happier than when she was with him.

"Wait, is he talking to Uncle Robert?" I cocked my head. Uncle Robert was Aunt Thelma's second husband, the one she'd been married to when I was a little girl, hence the title. I could never bring myself to drop it.

"I guess so. I had no idea Robert was even in town." Aunt Thelma fidgeted with her pearl bracelet.

"When's the last time you saw him?"

"Oh, years. Five at least." Aunt Thelma continued to watch the men converse. Her brow creased with worry. "If you'll excuse me. I'll be right back."

"I'll catch up with you later," I replied instead. If my aunt thought her guests would let her chat with me all night, she'd be mistaken. Everyone wanted a word with the woman of the hour. I continued scanning the room. I knew most of the people in attendance, but not everyone. Clemmie and Diane had overseen the guest list.

"Is that your uncle Robert?" My best friend, Misty, joined my side, handing me a sparkling glass of champagne.

"It is." We watched as Aunt Thelma joined the men's conversation. Both men's faces lit up when they saw her.

"It's been ages since I've seen him. Remember that time you put a frog in his boot?" Misty smiled.

"Only because you and Vance dared me to!" I

suddenly felt like I was ten years old again, and just as guilty.

"He never did find out it was you," Misty replied.

"Oh, he knew. He just didn't rat me out."

"I always did like him. It's a shame the marriage didn't work out."

"I know," I agreed with Misty.

"There you are," Vance said, joining us. "I was going to give this to you, but it looks like someone beat me to it." Vance held up an extra glass of champagne.

"Thank you. That was sweet of you." I kissed him on the cheek.

Misty sighed.

"What?" I questioned my best friend.

"You two are so cute."

"Stop," I shook my head and then took a drink. "Speaking of cute couples, where's Daniel?" I asked, referring to Misty's boyfriend.

"Oh, he had to step outside and take a call. The band's coming to town in a few weeks to work on the new album. He's still arranging it all."

"Oh, that's right. He reserved a block of rooms at the inn a while back."

Misty nodded and sipped her champagne. "He's trying to get them to cut the new album in town."

"That would be different." Daniel always had to

go where the music was, meaning leaving Misty behind, or she had to go on the road with him.

"It would be nice," Misty confessed.

Just then, the music shifted. A sudden swell of sound filled the room as the orchestra began to play a waltz. The notes moved together in a graceful dance, weaving in and out of each other, creating a beautiful melody.

"Care to dance?" Vance asked me.

I eyed the dance floor. A few couples seemed to know what they were doing, including Clemmie and her new boyfriend, Theo. She had met the man online, and this was their first time meeting in person. He was staying at the inn, and much to my surprise, he seemed like a nice man. I had been skeptical of Clemmie's online dating.

"I might step on your toes," I warned Vance as I watched Aunt Thelma and Frederick also join in the dance, moving gracefully across the floor.

"It's okay. I'll take my chances." Vance took my champagne glass and set it on the high top table behind us. He then took my hand and led me onto the dance floor where he pulled me close, his arm wrapped around my waist, and I placed my hand on his shoulder. As the music swelled, we began to move together.

At first, I stumbled a bit, trying to keep up with Vance's steps. But he was patient, guiding me through the dance with ease.

"You're a natural," he whispered in my ear as we spun around the dance floor.

"I just want to know where you learned to dance like this."

"I wanted to surprise you." That comment got a look out of me. "Who do you think requested the waltz?" Vance looked unapologetic. "We were so busy at our wedding that we hardly had time to dance. I thought you deserved one to never forget."

"Who knew you were so romantic?" I replied with a laugh.

In the soft light, the world around us faded away, leaving only Vance and me in our own magical bubble. Our feet moved to the music as if choreographed. Vance's eyes twinkled as he looked down at me, his arms wrapping gently around me as I melted into his embrace.

After the dance, we were forced back to reality. Boyd, the retired town attorney, pulled Vance into a conversation, and I found my way back to Misty, who was doing an awfully good job being a wallflower. It wasn't like Misty to be off in the corner. She was usually the life of the party.

"You're quiet tonight. Everything okay?" I asked, noticing my friend's distant gaze.

Misty turned to me with a small smile. "Yeah, everything's fine. I'm just ... I don't know, thinking about things, I guess."

"What things?" I pressed gently.

Misty hesitated for a moment, then leaned in to whisper to me. "I never thought I'd want to get married, you know? But seeing you and Vance so happy together... It's made me think differently."

My heart swelled with love for my best friend. "You know what they say. First comes love, then comes marriage, then comes—" I swayed while singing the classic children's rhyme.

"Stop!" Misty swatted at my arm, but I'd stepped out of range.

"Have you talked to Daniel about it?"

Misty shook her head. "Nooooo, and don't you dare bring it up. I don't want to scare him off or anything. And who knows, maybe it's just a passing phase."

I gave her a reassuring smile. "I don't know, maybe he's thinking the same thing. Just take it slow, and see where it goes." I shrugged.

"Probably with him running right out of town," Misty grumbled.

"Stop. He'll probably march you right down to the courthouse. You're a catch, and he knows it."

"Shhhh, don't say anything." Misty gave me a look as Daniel approached. "Everything okay?" she asked Daniel.

"Yeah." Daniel turned his attention to me. "Do you still have that block of rooms set aside?"

"I'm sure we do, but I'll confirm it to be on the safe side."

"Thank you, I appreciate it. The guys are coming in on the eighteenth."

"I'll text you from work tomorrow."

Daniel turned his attention to Misty. "I can't waltz like those two," Daniel nodded in my direction, "but I'd still love to dance with you."

"Well, since you asked nicely." Misty handed me her glass.

"Have fun, you two," I called out after them.

Ten minutes later, as I looked out at the sea of Regency-era costumes, an older man approached me. He stood tall and regal, with a commanding presence, as if he truly was a member of the British aristocracy.

"Excuse me," he said, his voice smooth and confident. "I couldn't help but notice how lovely this party is. Do you know who planned this event?" The man motioned to the sea of guests.

I turned to face him, taking in his striking features and immaculate appearance. He was dressed in a white shirt and black vest, with a coordinating top hat and silver-tipped cane. It was hard to tell if the cane was for support or decoration. "My friends and I arranged it," I said, smiling politely. "It was a lot of work, but we're really happy with how it turned out."

The man nodded appreciatively. "You did a wonderful job. Outstanding, really." He thumped his cane in approval.

"Thank you." I turned to walk away, but the man stopped me.

"I'm in the market for an event planner. Would you be interested in the position?"

"Oh." I laughed inwardly. Event planning used to be my life, but not anymore. "That's so kind of you." I thought my words through. I didn't want to offend the gentleman, but I had no intention of taking on any additional work. "I appreciate the offer, but that isn't something I do full-time. It was more of a one-off event."

"Well, I figured it couldn't hurt to ask." The man raised his drink to me in a salute. "Have a nice evening." He smiled, but the emotion didn't reach his eyes.

"Yes, you too."

As I turned away from the mysterious gentleman, I couldn't help but feel a sense of unease. There was something off-putting about him, but I couldn't quite put my finger on it.

Vance approached me, a concerned expression on his face. "Who was that?"

"I have no idea," I admitted. "He just came up to me and started talking about the party. He seemed impressed and wanted to hire me to plan some events."

Vance raised an eyebrow.

"Don't worry, I told him I wasn't interested, but I would like to find out who he is."

"He's not a local unless he's someone new."

I nodded in agreement. "He's not glowing either." Mortals glowed in Silverlake. It was how we witches knew not to perform magic in front of them.

Vance followed the man with his eyes. "He's a supernatural of some sort."

"And most likely a random friend of my aunt's. You should've seen the guest list. I think we capped it at three hundred."

"And all of them turned up."

"They sure did." It seemed even more people had packed into the ballroom if that was even possible. "We should probably keep the party moving."

"Do you want to get your aunt to cut the cake?"

"I think that's a good idea. Then after that, we can move on to her gifts."

Chapter 2

Aunt Thelma never did get a chance to open her gifts. There were just too many people, and the party took on a life of its own. The celebration would've continued all night long if the community center hadn't kicked us out at midnight. Personally, I was thankful they gave us the boot. I was dead on my feet and knew we had a ton of work ahead of us cleaning up the place.

"Do you just want to come back in the morning?" Libby, the community center manager, had motioned to the discarded cups, stained tablecloths, and half-deflated balloons.

"Yes, yes, we would," I had replied. Which was where we were going to head this morning after having brunch with Aunt Thelma and a few friends while she opened her gifts.

"Anyone else want some cake?" Clemmie called

out from my aunt's kitchen while taking down a stack of plates from the cupboard. The remnants of the towering masterpiece sat on my aunt's dining room table. Diane had outdone herself. The cake had spanned several tiers and had been adorned with intricate fondant flowers and gold swirls, adding to the regal atmosphere of the party. The base layer had been a rich, decadent chocolate cake, followed by a layer of velvety red cake and then a layer of light and fluffy vanilla cake. Each layer had been separated by a generous spread of creamy frosting flavored with hints of vanilla and almond extract. It had been the perfect centerpiece for the celebration, and its sweet aroma now wafted through the apartment, enticing me to take a slice even though I hadn't had breakfast yet.

"Who wants french toast?" Vance's mom, Heather, interrupted, walking in the unlatched door and balancing two large trays. Heather owned the diner in town, famous for its large portions and all-American favorites.

"Here, Mom, let me help," Vance stepped forward and took the trays.

"One's French toast. The other is bacon. I have the eggs in my car."

"I'll lend you a hand," I offered. Aunt Thelma's apartment was on the third floor of Mystic Inn. Heather had gotten her workout in carrying up the first two trays.

"Thanks, sweetie," Heather replied as I followed her out the apartment door.

Forty-five minutes later, we'd all stuffed ourselves silly with Heather's cooking and Diane's cake. If we didn't wrap this impromptu feast up soon, I'd need to head home for a nap before cleaning up the community center.

"Did I tell you how lovely you looked last night?" Frederick said to my aunt as they walked their plates into the kitchen.

"Only a time or two." My aunt blushed.

"Well, it bears repeating," Frederick remarked.

I smiled at the exchange and headed back into the living room. When they returned, I noticed I wasn't the only one ready to wrap things up. Clemmie and Diane were standing over the pile of gifts taking over the corner of the room.

"Do you want to write down who gave what?" Diane asked.

"And I'll hand the gifts to her," Clemmie nodded.

"Thelma, come over here and have a seat," Diane instructed as my aunt and Frederick walked back from the kitchen.

Aunt Thelma made her way over to the pile of gifts and sat down in her favorite armchair. Clemmie and Diane took their places on either side of her, with the pile of presents in front of them.

Diane began to pass gifts over, announcing who the gift was from, while Clemmie took notes.

Luke and the twins' gift was a box of hand-made chocolate truffles from The Candy Cauldron, each one decorated with intricate swirls of chocolate, and knowing the twins, packed with unique flavor combinations. Connie, the owner of the local potion shop, had sent a spa package, complete with scented candles, magical bath salts, and a fluffy white robe. A note attached to the package apologized for Connie's absence from the party, explaining that she had to work at the shop. Clemmie's gift was a box of custom-designed teas, each one labeled with a witty name like "Regency Romance" and "Mrs. Darcy's Delight." Diane's gift was a beautiful antique hand mirror, which she had carefully restored herself. Vance and I had bought Aunt Thelma an enchanted bottle of perfume.

As Aunt Thelma opened our gift, she looked at us with a warm smile. "Oh my, this is lovely," she said as she admired the intricately designed bottle. "What kind of perfume is it?"

"That magical kind," I explained. "It changes scents based on your mood."

Aunt Thelma spritzed the perfume on her wrist. Even from afar, I smelled the scent of fresh-cut grass mixed with lavender. In other words, summertime in a bottle.

Aunt Thelma looked impressed. "How lovely. Thank you so much, dear."

Diane then handed over a small, rectangular-shaped present. From the outside, it looked like jewelry or maybe a pen set if the gift wasn't as generous as it first appeared.

"Is this from you?" Aunt Thelma looked over at Frederick.

"No, I'm afraid not. I was saving your gift for your actual birthday tomorrow."

"Who's this from?" Aunt Thelma asked Diane.

"I'm not sure. I didn't see a card." Diane and Clemmie looked at the surrounding discarded wrapping paper but came up empty.

"Must've lost it along the way," Clemmie remarked.

Aunt Thelma shrugged and carefully opened the gift. Inside was a velvet box. She clicked it open, revealing a stunning necklace. The pendant was a delicate, intricately crafted rose made of gold and encrusted with diamonds. Aunt Thelma's eyes widened at the sight of it.

"Well, whomever it's from, it's beautiful," Aunt Thelma reluctantly admitted.

My mind instantly went to my former uncle Robert. He had been known to dote on my aunt with expensive gifts when they were married. I wondered if my aunt thought the same thing. I wouldn't dare ask her in front of Frederick.

Aunt Thelma put her hand under the necklace, so the pendant was cradled in her palm, and peered closer at it.

An instant later, she slumped forward, passing out.

"Thelma!" Frederick called her name, rushing forward.

Aunt Thelma would have fallen right out of the chair if Clemmie hadn't caught her. The velvet box fell out of her hand and landed on the carpet.

I stood there momentarily stunned. This was why I wasn't a full-time sheriff deputy. Sometimes I froze when under pressure. Like right now, I couldn't even move. My friends moved around me as if in slow motion, each one rising to the occasion. Solving cases was one thing, but being thrown into adrenaline-inducing situations on the regular was something entirely different.

"Lean her back!" Clemmie instructed. Diane was right there before Frederick. She helped push Aunt Thelma back until she was resting against the back of the chair, but she was still out cold.

Frederick took her pulse. "Her pulse is strong," he said, staring at Aunt Thelma.

Clemmie leaned in close. "Thelma, you have to wake up. Do you hear me?"

It was only then that I snapped out of it. "I'll call for an ambulance," I called out. I reached for my phone, but I saw that Vance was already on his.

"That's right. Thelma Nightingale. Third floor of Mystic Inn. She's out cold." Vance was quiet while he listened to the question on the other end. "No, we don't know what happened," he said the last part to me.

"Do you think it's the necklace?" I hissed. We looked at each other, eyes wide with the realization. "Don't touch that!" I shouted as Diane went to pick up the box. "It might be cursed."

Diane jumped back.

Vance was busy filling the operator in on the potentially cursed object. "It was a gift. A necklace. She'd just opened it before passing out. It might not be it, but..." Again, Vance was silent. "Yes, that's probably a good idea." Vance put his hand over the receiver portion of his phone. "They're calling the sheriff," he explained.

"Okay." I looked nervously over at my aunt. She was still knocked out, despite everyone's best efforts. Heather ran into the kitchen and wetted a washcloth, placing the cool cloth on my aunt's forehead.

Vance hung up the phone. "They're on their way."

I nodded.

"Are you okay?" he asked.

I couldn't answer. I was numb. For a long time, it had only been Aunt Thelma and me. What if it was her heart? What if she had a stroke? I wasn't sure what ailment was worse. A health emergency or a cursed artifact. I couldn't voice my concerns. "She has to be okay," I whispered.

As we waited for the paramedics to arrive, Percy the Poltergeist floated into the room. Despite his mischievous tendencies, he loved Aunt Thelma as much as I did.

"What did you do?!" Percy seemed panicky, and he never panicked.

"Nothing! We're not sure what happened." My voice was louder, and my tone higher than usual.

"Where's Eleanor? I need to find Eleanor," Percy looked about the room for his ghostly wife.

"Listen, before you take off, do me a favor." Percy's eyes locked with mine. "I'm going to go with Aunt Thelma to the hospital. Keep an eye on things while we're gone. I'll call you as soon as I know something."

"You got it, Jelly!" Percy saluted before disappearing through the wall.

The paramedics arrived a few minutes later and quickly took charge. Heather had thought ahead and moved presents and the wrappings out of the way to give them room to maneuver.

"Everyone, please step back," one of the paramedics said in a firm but professional tone. I hadn't realized how tightly we were hovering.

We backed up to give them space, watching anxiously as they assessed Aunt Thelma's condition. The second paramedic called out vital signs to his partner as they ran through their checklist. "Blood pressure is 120 over 80, oxygen saturation is at 97%, heart rate is steady at 70 beats per minute," he reported.

The first paramedic turned to us and offered some reassurance. "Her vitals are strong, but we need to get her to the hospital for further evaluation. We're going to administer some oxygen and start an IV to keep her hydrated. We'll also do an electrocardiograph to check for any heart irregularities."

"Thank you," I said, feeling grateful for their quick response.

As the paramedics worked, Diane called Cassidy, one of the town's healers, to fill her in on what happened. "She's stopping by the apartment to pick up the necklace and is then going to meet Thelma at the hospital," Diane announced. We all knew that if it was a magical ailment, she was our best chance at a full recovery.

"ECG looks normal," the paramedic informed us. "We're going to go ahead and get her to the hospital."

"I'm coming with you," Frederick announced before I could. I couldn't help my shocked expression. I wasn't used to being second to anyone in my aunt's life.

"We'll follow you over," Vance announced, reaching for my purse.

"Thanks," I replied to my husband, meeting his eyes.

"We'll wait here for Cassidy," Diane reassured me.

"And I'll clean up all the food," Heather added.

"Thank you all," I said over my shoulder while following the paramedics out. We couldn't get to the hospital soon enough.

Chapter 3

At the hospital, things moved at a painstakingly slow pace. Aunt Thelma was taken back for tests to try to determine the cause of her unconscious state. Frederick was also there with us in the waiting room. He looked heartbroken as we awaited the results. His eyes were sad and distant, as though his thoughts were far away.

Finally, after what felt like an eternity, the doctor came back with his initial assessment. "Physically, she appears to be in excellent health." Dr. Parrish flipped through Aunt Thelma's chart. I didn't know the young doctor all that well other than he was Mayor Parrish's nephew, as our mayor would tell anyone who would listen. *We're so lucky he decided to practice here!* She said over and over again. "No signs of trauma, no underlying conditions, all her vitals are normal," Dr. Parrish continued.

"Does that mean she was cursed?" I asked anxiously.

"It's too early to say for sure. We're still ruling out any neurological issues."

"Like a stroke?" Frederick asked.

The doctor nodded. "We'll know more when we get the results back from her neurological evaluation."

I nodded, feeling helpless. Vance squeezed my hand reassuringly.

"Cassidy is analyzing the necklace, but I expect she'll be in soon," Dr. Parrish added.

I nodded, unable to speak.

"Can we see her?" Vance asked on my behalf.

"Yes, you can. She's just getting back from an MRI. I'll let you know when we get those results."

We thanked the doctor and followed his directions to Aunt Thelma's room. When we walked in, the room was still and silent. It was hard to see Aunt Thelma hooked up to machines and monitors.

I reached out and took her hand, willing her to wake up. "I don't know what's happened to you. But we're going to figure it out, okay?"

Vance placed a hand on my shoulder as Frederick came around and joined us on the other side of the bed. "Let's sit with her for a while," he said softly.

We settled into the chairs next to her bed. Frederick wiped his eyes and squeezed Aunt Thelma's hand tightly, letting her know that he was there too.

I sat there silently, watching her chest rise and fall with the rhythm of the machines.

The minutes ticked by, and there was still no change in her status.

My phone buzzed a couple of hours later. It was a text from Clemmie. It read: *Hey, how's Thelma doing?*

I sighed and typed out a response: *No change. We're still at the hospital.*

A few moments later, my phone buzzed again. *I have the gang together at the tea shop. Come join us if you need a break.*

I wasn't planning on going anywhere and was about to tell Clemmie as much when Dr. Parrish knocked on the door and poked his head in.

"How are you doing?" he said, keeping his voice low.

"We're okay," I replied. Given the circumstances, I added to myself.

The doctor walked in the rest of the way and took a seat across from us. "I have all the test results back. Everything appears to be normal, so we can rule out any physical ailments or injuries."

"That means she was cursed?" Frederick asked.

"Looks like it," the doctor confirmed.

I wasn't sure how I felt. Relief and anger warred in my heart. The stress of the morning caught up with me, and a sob bubbled out of my mouth. I couldn't understand who would want to curse her. It didn't make sense.

"We're going to figure this out," Vance said, squeezing my hand and kissing my cheek. "I promise."

I nodded and tried to swallow around the lump in my throat. We had to find out who did this and why. Aunt Thelma deserved justice.

WE HEADED to Clemmie's shop to fill the gang in on Aunt Thelma and start our investigation. Frederick stayed back at the hospital. He promised he'd call as soon as something changed.

When we arrived at the shop, everyone was already deep in conversation about what might have happened to Aunt Thelma. Misty's brow furrowed as she speculated that Aunt Thelma might have had a stroke while Daniel nodded in agreement. Clemmie was convinced it was a curse. Longtime friends, Roger and Diane, weren't sure what had happened, but they wanted to help in any way they could.

"Well, Clemmie's right. It was a curse." I took a seat at one of the small tables.

"I knew it. Thelma's as healthy as a horse. Nothing short of a wallop of dark magic would knock her out." Clemmie placed a cup of tea in front of me and Vance. The tea smelled of honey with a hint of orange. I took a sip. The warm liquid slid down my throat and calmed me from the inside out. It was no doubt infused with some sort of soothing potion.

Vance and I then filled our friends in on the doctor's diagnosis, but no one could explain why Aunt Thelma had been cursed.

"Everyone loves Thelma," Diane said.

"Who would do such a thing?" Roger looked downright distraught.

"I don't know," I replied.

"I think we should start by looking into Thelma's past," Misty suggested. "It could provide some clues."

"I agree. That's our best bet," Vance replied.

"There were a ton of people there last night. Misty told me about your uncle," Daniel added.

I nodded, remembering Uncle Robert. Could he have done such a thing? I looked over at Clemmie to see what she thought, but she was surprisingly quiet as she moved around the room, silently refilling everyone's cups. Clemmie looked lost in thought as she circled the table, her eyes distant and her movements slow and deliberate. Meanwhile, Diane took out a folded piece of paper. It looked like a spreadsheet. I realized it was the guest list. She turned it toward Roger, and the two began looking it over.

"Everyone on here is her friend," Diane said more to herself than anyone.

"I think I know who might have done this," Clemmie finally spoke up after she finished pouring tea for everyone.

"Who?" Misty and I asked in unison.

"An ex-business partner of Aunt Thelma's," Clemmie replied. "He was a part of the inn when things weren't doing so great." I went to interrupt, but Clemmie shushed me. "You were living in Chicago at the time." My aunt's best friend gave me a level stare. I pressed my lips closed. I didn't like to be reminded how I'd abandoned my aunt for all those years, but I couldn't deny it either.

"Who's the business partner?" Vance brought the conversation back around.

"Ivan Ansel. They never actually formed a partnership, and that's when things turned sour. You saw him last night, Angelica. I saw the two of you talking."

I stared at Clemmie, trying to figure out who she was talking about.

"Top hat, walked with a fancy cane," Clemmie supplied.

"That guy! Oh, I didn't catch his name." I turned to Vance. "Remember the man that asked me about event planning?"

"I knew I didn't like him," Vance replied.

"I don't know all the details, but Thelma wasn't happy to see him last night. She flat out ignored him when he tried to talk with her," Clemmie remarked.

"I don't remember seeing him before," I said.

"That's because he doesn't live here full-time," Roger replied.

"He has a summer home on the other side of the lake," Diane added. "I don't think he even opens it up every year."

That explained it. "What about Uncle Robert?" I asked Clemmie. "He's who first came to mind when I saw the necklace. Remember how he always gave her jewelry?"

"I suppose he should be a suspect, too," Clemmie agreed.

"I can see him being one of those if-I-can't-have-her-no-one-else-can-either types," Roger weighed in.

"That's a good point," Vance agreed. "But I doubt he'd do something as extreme as this."

"I don't know. Roger makes a good point. Robert was head over heels in love with Thelma. If he's back in town, it can only mean one thing," Clemmie replied.

"We should talk to him," I said to Vance.

"What about Elizabeth Conner?" Diane looked up from her list.

"Who's Elizabeth?" Daniel asked.

Clemmie and Diane looked at each other knowingly. "Elizabeth was Thelma's friend slash enemy in high school," Clemmie said.

Diane nodded her head in recognition. "It was so strange seeing her again last night after all these years."

"I wonder if that's whom Aunt Thelma meant?" I said out loud.

"When?" Clemmie asked.

"We were briefly talking, and Aunt Thelma said, *I wonder what she's doing here?* But then she saw Frederick, and she changed the subject.

"What *was* she doing there?" Diane asked curiously.

"I don't know. I don't remember seeing her name on the invite list, and I mailed them all out."

"I don't know, either," Clemmie replied, shaking her head. "I wasn't expecting to see her there either. She wasn't on the guest list."

"That's what I thought," I remarked.

The group exchanged glances, unsure of what to make of Elizabeth's unexpected attendance. We had all heard stories about how Elizabeth and Thelma constantly fought during their high school days, and it seemed like they hadn't made peace since then, either.

"Roger and I can go and pay a visit," Diane offered.

"I'll go with—" Clemmie abruptly stopped talking. "Is that? No, it can't be..." Clemmie leaned forward and squinted as she looked out her shop's front window. "Quick, cover for me!" she whispered before dashing behind the counter and ducking down.

"What in the world?" Diane swiveled in her seat as Clemmie scurried to hide.

None of us knew what Clemmie was talking about.

"Clemmie, what are you—" Misty started to say.

"Shhhh! Don't say anything," Clemmie hissed.

A moment later, a handsome older man I'd never seen before walked into the shop. The man had a kind face, with a hint of worry in his eyes as he scanned the shop. He held a bouquet of wildflowers in a firm grip. His clothing was well fitted and fashionable but not overly showy. A golden watch shone on his left wrist, and his hair was neatly combed to the side.

Misty stood and readily filled in as an employee. "Good afternoon, welcome to Sit For A Spell. How can I help you?" The rest of us tried to act like customers having a lovely afternoon tea, but it was hard not to stare.

The man's gaze finally landed on Misty. He cleared his throat before speaking. "Good afternoon. I'm looking for Clemmie. Is she here?"

Misty shook her head. "I'm sorry. Clemmie isn't here right now," she said apologetically.

The man's face fell in disappointment, but he kept his composure. "Do you know where I might find her?" he asked hopefully.

Misty shook her head again. "I'm afraid not, but I'd be happy to pass on a message if you'd like."

The man thanked her kindly and set down the bouquet of wildflowers. "Do you have a pen?"

"Oh, sure," Misty walked behind the counter where Clemmie was hiding and bent low to retrieve a pen and paper. Clemmie scootched further into the alcove. The man followed but stayed on the other side of the counter.

He wrote quickly, the pen scratching against the paper as he formed each word. After a few moments, he folded the paper into thirds and tucked it into the bouquet of wildflowers. "Please tell her that I wanted to surprise her, but I suppose a note will have to do," he said in a gentle voice.

"I'll be sure she gets this," Misty replied.

The man thanked Misty for her help before turning around and walking out of the shop.

Clemmie seemed to count to ten before emerging. She rose slowly to her feet and smoothed her shirt, peering out the window in the process. We all stared at her, waiting for an explanation.

"Well?" Diane finally asked after Clemmie still hadn't spoken.

"Well, what?" Clemmie replied nonchalantly.

"Oh, come on!" Misty exclaimed. "Who was that man? And why were you hiding?"

Clemmie hesitated for a moment before finally sighing, "Fine." My best friend took a deep breath and looked around the room at all of us. "That was Carl," she said softly. "We met online."

"And?" We all knew there was more to the story.

"And I'm just surprised to see him, that's all," Clemmie replied with a fake smile as if she hadn't just been hiding under the counter.

"You didn't know he was in town," Misty surmised.

Diane's eyes went wide. "He stalked you?"

Clemmie grimaced. "Something like that."

"What?!" Vance said at the same time Daniel and Roger stood. The trio of men walked to the door and stepped outside, no doubt trying to find Carl.

"Get back here!" Clemmie shouted. "Carl's harmless. At least I think he is," she said the second part to herself. "Don't worry about him. We've got bigger fish to fry."

"Still, Clemmie, I don't like this," Diane spoke up. "How did he find you?"

"I'm not sure. I don't think I even told him where I lived," Clemmie confessed.

I jumped in before I could help myself. "See! What did I tell you? Online dating is the worst. I told you to be careful."

"Hush now. Carl's a nice guy, if not a bit overeager." Clemmie tried to act like she wasn't bothered by the man's sudden appearance, but we all knew better. She lifted the note out of the flowers and quickly read it. "He's staying in town at your place," Clemmie looked up at me. By my place, she meant Mystic Inn.

"You want me to get rid of him?" I'd never kicked someone out of the inn who didn't deserve it, but I'd be willing to if the man were a stalker. All I would have to do was fill Percy in, and he'd make the man's life so miserable he'd check out on his own. Have you ever tried to take a shower while a poltergeist serenaded you?

"No, no, not yet." Clemmie looked thoughtful.

"Isn't Theo staying at the inn too?" Misty asked.

"Shoot, you're right. How could I've have forgotten about Theo? We were supposed to meet for lunch, but then everything happened with Thelma, and I completely forgot." Clemmie closed her eyes. "How did I end up with two men in town?" she groaned.

I opened my mouth to answer, but Misty shot me a look. Now wasn't the time to harp on Clemmie's online dating life. I'd already done that enough.

"While Clemmie's figuring out her love life, I say we get down to business," Roger suggested. "Diane and I will head to Elizabeth's."

"I have to head to work, but I can give you a hand at the inn later if you'd like me to cover a shift," Misty offered.

"Thank you. I might take you up on that. Percy's covering things for now, but I hate to leave him in charge indefinitely."

Misty nodded.

"I can help with research," Daniel offered.

"I appreciate that," Vance said.

"I'll write down a list of names. Let's see if we can get some background information on Elizabeth, Mr. Ansel, and my Uncle Robert," I said. Daniel nodded. "Vance and I will visit the men in person, and then maybe we can all meet back up?"

Everyone agreed that was a good plan. "I'll text everyone," I suggested. We chatted frequently enough that we already had a group message set up. With all the cases we'd solved, there was nothing we couldn't handle. "Let's get to work."

Chapter 4

Vance and I decided to start our investigation with dapper Mr. Ansel. Diane was able to provide further directions to his home, with Roger clarifying that it was more of a hunting lodge than a house. I wasn't sure what he meant by that, but I was intrigued, nonetheless.

As we drove around the lake toward Mr. Ansel's "hunting lodge" I couldn't help but feel a sense of unease. The trees were tall and dense, casting deep shadows over the dirt road we followed. My magical intuition tingled, and while I didn't want to come across as paranoid, I did want to be ready for whatever came our way.

When we finally arrived at the lodge, I could see why Roger had described it as such. It was a large, wooden structure that looked like it belonged in the middle of a deep forest, not mere miles from our village. The air was thick with the scent of pine. My ears pricked up, listening for any subtle noises that might indicate a threat. A distant hoot of an owl, the crackle of a twig underfoot—anything hinting at impending danger.

As we approached the door, I could see that it was made of thick, carved wood and had a brass knocker in the shape of a deer's head.

Vance knocked on the door, and we waited. After a few moments, the door creaked open, and a tall, elderly man with a neatly trimmed mustache and a tweed jacket appeared. He looked us up and down, his eyes lingering on our wands, before finally speaking.

"Can I help you?" the butler asked, his voice deep and gravelly.

"Is Mr. Ansel available?" Vance asked.

"Regarding?" The butler's expression remained unchanged.

"We have a few questions about a recent gathering he attended." I wasn't sure what else to say. There was no way the butler would let us in if we told him we wanted to interview his boss.

"Do you have a card?" The butler looked down his nose at us.

I looked at Vance. I didn't regularly carry business cards, but I knew Vance did. He pulled a card out of his wallet and handed it over.

"You can tell Mr. Ansel that we spoke last night

at the party. I'm the event planner," I added, hoping that little detail might help us gain entry.

"Please wait here a moment." The butler shut the door.

"Well, this is interesting," Vance remarked.

"Who knew he had a butler? Fancy."

Before Vance could reply, the butler was back at the door.

"Mr. Ansel will see you now." The butler looked at us for a moment longer, then stepped back to allow us inside. The interior of the lodge was just as rustic as the exterior, with wooden beams and hardwood floors. The air was thick with the scent of woodsmoke and old books.

Mr. Ansel was in a brown leather armchair by the burning fire, sipping on a whiskey despite it being the middle of the day. He easily rose to meet us without a cane in sight, his bright blue eyes examining me from head to toe.

"How delightful to see you again. I take it you have reconsidered my offer from last night?"

I quickly shook my head. "No, actually, I was hoping you could help us with something else."

Mr. Ansel's expression faltered, but he quickly recovered. "I can certainly try. Would you like something to drink?" Mr. Ansel said the last part to his butler, who magically appeared in the doorway. I learned a long time ago that people tended to open up more over drinks, but that didn't mean I was about to sip on a whiskey before noon.

"Tea?" I suggested.

Mr. Ansel turned to Vance for his order.

"Tea would be great," Vance agreed.

The butler nodded and disappeared into the other room. A few moments later, he returned with a tray of tea and cookies. I'd bet any money the butler had conjured the tray from somewhere, given how quickly it materialized. Vance took a piece of shortbread off the silver platter while I doctored our teas.

Mr. Ansel took a seat opposite us, ready to answer our questions.

"What can I help you with?" he asked after we all sat and took a sip of our respective drinks.

"It's about my aunt. You two know each other well, I understand?" I asked, getting straight to the point.

Mr. Ansel's eyes flickered with surprise. "Yes, Thelma and I have been friends for years. Why do you ask?"

"We were hoping you could shed some light on a recent curse."

"A curse?" Mr. Ansel looked between Vance and I for clarification.

"My aunt was cursed after her party," I explained.

Mr. Ansel's face fell. He took a long sip of

whiskey before replying, as if he was buying himself time. "This is the first I've heard of it. She looked lovely on Saturday night. What happened?"

"It was one of the gifts," I purposely left the details vague. "We're still trying to figure out who gave it to her."

"I see," Mr. Ansel said, his eyes narrowing slightly. "I'm sorry to hear about your aunt. But I can assure you, I had nothing to do with it."

"But you two do have history, correct? Something to do with a business deal?" Vance asked.

"You had a falling out?" I pressed on.

Mr. Ansel sighed, leaning back in his chair. "I'm not sure I'd call it a falling out."

"What would you call it?" Vance asked.

Mr. Ansel thought of the right word. "A disagreement. But it was nothing serious. Thelma can be quite stubborn at times, as I'm sure you know. And I certainly wouldn't resort to such petty measures as cursing someone."

"Of course," I said smoothly. "But could you tell us more about this disagreement? It might help us in our investigation."

Mr. Ansel hesitated for a moment, then sighed. "Very well. Thelma and I were in talks about a potential business merger. But we couldn't come to an agreement on terms, so we decided to end the negotiations. That was all."

I nodded, taking a sip of my tea.

"Do you know if Thelma was in talks with anyone else?" Vance asked.

Mr. Ansel raised an eyebrow. "I'm not sure. I don't keep tabs on her business dealings."

"Understandable," Vance said, his tone nonchalant.

"Do you know of anyone who might have a motive to harm her?" I asked.

Mr. Ansel frowned, taking another sip of his whiskey. "No, I can't say that I do. From my understanding, Thelma is a beloved member of the community. I can't imagine anyone wanting to harm her."

"But?" I could tell there was more.

After a few moments of silence, Mr. Ansel cleared his throat. "But I can think of more than one person who'd want to hurt that boyfriend of hers."

"Mr. Frederick?" I replied.

Mr. Ansel paused, his gaze shifting out the window to the darkened sky. Clouds had gathered, a billowy mass of gray and black. A thunderstorm was brewing. Lightning flickered in the distance. The heavens would open any moment now. "Do you know how many people are upset he's not Mount Holly's mayor anymore?" Mr. Ansel referenced the magical Christmas village, which celebrated Yuletide year-round, and where Mr. Frederick had been mayor for years. Like Silverlake, the town thrived on tourism. "Rumor has it your aunt talked him into early retirement. Now the town's falling apart, and it's all her fault. Trust me, people don't like it when they start losing money."

I paused to take another sip of my tea, considering Mr. Ansel's words carefully. His reasoning was sound: before Aunt Thelma arrived, Mr. Frederick had been content running the Christmas village, but this was the first time I'd heard rumors of something awry in that area.

Thunder rumbled in the distance. We were going to have to cut our visit short or wait out the storm, and I didn't want to do that if we could help it.

"Thank you for your time and your input, Mr. Ansel. We appreciate it," I said, rising from my chair.

Vance did the same. "We'll be in touch if we have any further questions."

"Of course," Mr. Ansel nodded, his expression grave. "If there's anything else I can do to help, don't hesitate to let me know."

As we made our way out of the lodge, the storm finally broke. Rain poured down in sheets. In a matter of seconds, both Vance and I were drenched. So much for trying to beat the storm. We laughed despite ourselves as we ran back to the truck, sharing looks of resignation as we hopped in.

Despite the noise and chaos, I couldn't help but

think about Mr. Ansel's words. He had brought up an interesting point: could someone from Mount Holly have been angry enough with Frederick to harm Aunt Thelma? It was something to consider as we continued our investigation into who was behind her attack.

"Well, that was interesting," Vance said, backing out of the driveway.

"I think we need to talk to Mr. Frederick," I said, my mind already racing with possibilities.

Vance nodded, his eyes on the road "And we need to find out more about this potential merger between Aunt Thelma and Mr. Ansel's businesses. It's possible that someone from Mr. Ansel's camp could have something to do with the curse."

"That's a good point." I hadn't thought of that.

"I'll dig into Mr. Ansel's team background and see what I can find out," Vance offered.

"Let's get a list of names from Frederick, too," I agreed.

As we drove back to Silverlake, the rain pounded against the windshield, and the wind howled outside. It was as if the storm was trying to warn us of the danger that lay ahead.

But I wasn't about to let a little weather slow us down.

Chapter 5

We were almost back home when my mind snapped back to the community center. I groaned. "We completely forgot to go back and clean up after the party!" I felt awful. "I know we have a lot on our mind, but we told Libby we'd clean up. She probably hates us by now."

"Are you kidding me? She's probably more worried about Aunt Thelma. You know everyone in town knows about it by now."

Vance was right. You couldn't keep things quiet in a small town.

"Still, we should go back and offer to help." I snapped my fingers, my brain finally working right. "We should also see if they have security cameras. What time is it?" I glanced at the clock; it was going on six. "The center's still open for another couple of hours."

"Okay, let's head there."

We made our way back to the community center and spotted Libby as soon as we stepped through the doors.

"How's Thelma? Is she okay?" the manager asked me before I could even say I was sorry.

Vance gave me a knowing smile.

"She's still unconscious as far as I know. We're going to head there next." I looked at Vance to see if that was okay with him. He nodded.

"Don't worry about anything here. I got it all taken care of. You two go be with your family." Libby gave me a reassuring smile.

"Are you sure?" I asked.

"We already cleaned everything up hours ago," Libby explained.

"Thank you. I feel awful dumping all of that on you," I confessed.

"Don't worry, we completely understand. Everyone does," Libby replied.

"Thank you. I owe you for sure," I replied.

"Careful, I might take you up on that. I need someone to help plan a charity gala next month. We're raising money for the new youth center."

"Absolutely, I'm happy to help."

"Really?" Libby seemed surprised.

"Sure, it sounds like a good cause."

"And speaking of good causes, Angie and I were

hoping you could help us with something else," Vance said.

Libby looked at us expectantly.

"Does the community center have any security cameras?" I asked.

Libby gestured around the hallway with her hand, pointing out the small cameras in the ceiling that overlooked all the entrances and exits. "We have a few. Mostly on the entrances and back offices."

"Are they in the ballroom?" I asked.

"Ballroom, no. Why?" Libby put two and two together. Her eyes widened at the implication. "Someone hurt your aunt on purpose? I thought it was a health scare."

It turned out the gossip mill hadn't caught up with the whole story. "She was cursed," I said, my voice lowered to a whisper. "By a necklace she received as a birthday gift."

Libby gasped. "That's terrible. I'm so sorry."

"Do you mind if we take a look at the footage?" Vance asked.

"Of course not. Let me show you where the control room is." Libby led us down a corridor to a small room with banks of monitors and recording equipment. "The cameras are on a loop, so I'll need to rewind the footage to the time you're interested in. What time are we looking for?"

I looked at Vance and answered, "Probably

when most of the guests arrived?"

"Got it." Libby rewound the footage, her fingers deftly working the controls. She stopped the playback and pointed at the screen. "There's your aunt, coming in with the other guests."

We watched as Aunt Thelma entered the ballroom, greeting people and chatting with friends. She looked happy and relaxed like she didn't have a care in the world.

Vance leaned in closer to the screen. "Can you zoom in on the doorway?"

"I can try," Libby worked the controls, zooming in.

The footage showed hundreds of party guests coming and going in their elaborate Regency outfits. Some of the ladies had intricate gowns with billowing skirts and ornate headdresses, while the gentlemen were dressed in waistcoats and breeches. There seemed to be a lot of laughter and conversation as everyone milled about. Unfortunately, we couldn't hear anything. There was no audio, just video. I watched for a few moments until Libby pointed out Aunt Thelma again. This time she was dressed in the gown we'd picked out for her.

"There she is," Libby said. We watched as Aunt Thelma moved through the crowd, stopping every now and then to chat with someone or admire a costume. Diane and Roger walk in next, arm in arm, with a large gift in hand. The same went for

Luke with his chocolates and dozens of other guests who walked through the doors with gifts in tow.

I sighed.

"This is going to take some time," Vance replied, reading my mind.

"You said it's a necklace?" Libby asked, leaning forward.

I thought back to what the gift had looked like before Aunt Thelma opened it. "It was wrapped in dark blue paper."

"With a gold bow, right?" Vance added.

"Yeah. I remember thinking it was jewelry or a pen set. It was small and rectangular like that."

"Okay, why don't I stay here and keep going through this," Libby offered.

"Are you sure? I hate to ask after you cleaned up everything," I protested.

"Honestly, your aunt is a lovely woman. It's the least I can do."

"Let her help," Vance replied.

I relented. "Okay, but only if you're sure. Do you know what my Uncle Robert looks like?"

Libby bit her lip in thought. "Was he wearing a bottle green coat and tan pants last night?"

I pointed at her. "Yes, that's him.

"What about Mr. Ansel?" Vance asked.

"Him, I know." Libby rolled her eyes. "He usually sends his butler to get fresh towels for the sauna."

"Maybe keep a close eye on those two," I said, motioning to the cameras.

Vance turned to me. "Who was the other person Diane mentioned? Elizabeth something?"

"Oh, Elizabeth Connor," I replied. "Do you know her?"

"She plays tennis here every Friday," Libby confirmed.

"Can you see what gift she brought?" I asked.

"Sure, I'll watch the footage and make some notes," Libby replied.

"It's a long shot, but you never know." After all, what was the chance the culprit waltzed into the community center with the cursed gift right out in the open?

"I'll give you a call after I go through it all," Libby promised, already fully engrossed in the task at hand.

As we left the community center, Vance put his arm around me. "I have a feeling Libby will find something useful," he said.

"I hope so. I hated seeing Aunt Thelma like that today."

"Do you still want to head back to the hospital?"

"I do. Even though I don't like it, I want to be there for her. Maybe Charity's figured the curse out." I looked down at my phone. I hadn't heard from anyone, so it was unlikely Aunt Thelma was awake, but I wanted to talk with the healer myself.

Chapter 6

We drove to the hospital in silence, both of us lost in our thoughts. I kept worrying about what we'd find when we arrived. When we finally pulled into the parking lot, the sun was starting to set. We hurried inside and took the elevator up to Aunt Thelma's room.

Charity met us outside of the room.

"How is she?" I asked.

"Still asleep, but I think I may have figured out how to break the curse," she said slowly.

"Really? That's great. How?" My words were laced with excitement and relief. Hopefully, this nightmare would soon be over.

"That's the tricky part. The necklace carries a powerful enchantment that can only be broken by the one who cast it."

My gaze dropped to the ground. If only we

knew who that person was. The hope I had moments ago was replaced by quiet despair.

"I take it you still don't know who that is?" Charity correctly read my expression.

"We're working on it, but no, not yet," Vance admitted.

Charity put a comforting hand on my shoulder. "Until you do, I've given her something that might help."

"What's that?" I asked.

"It's a potion to help alleviate some of the symptoms of the curse," she explained. "It didn't break the curse, but it should make her more comfortable. More like she's having a nice, refreshing nap."

I nodded, feeling grateful for Charity's help. "Thank you so much."

"It's the least I can do," Charity replied, her expression serious.

We said our goodbyes and went into Aunt Thelma's room. Frederick had dosed off but woke up when we entered.

"How's she doing?" I whispered.

"Better, I think. Charity gave her something."

"Yeah, we spoke with her in the hallway."

Aunt Thelma was still sleeping, but she looked more peaceful than she had earlier. "It looks like she's doing better," I said.

Frederick nodded. "When we find out who did

this—" He paused; his gaze focused on me. "Do you have any idea? Any leads?"

"That's something we wanted to talk to you about. Mr. Ansel mentioned that some people are upset you're not the mayor of Mount Holly anymore," I said.

Frederick looked like he wasn't following me.

"He made it seem like this attack might be against you," Vance explained.

Frederick's expression darkened. "I knew there were people upset with me, but I never thought anyone would go this far."

"Do you have any enemies in particular?" I asked.

"None that come to mind. I always tried to do what was best for the town."

"Which is why people are now upset. I'm not sure who the new mayor is, but it sounds like things aren't going so well," I said.

"I never thought my political career would lead to something like this."

"It's not your fault," I assured him.

"That's kind of you to say, but if it is someone from Mount Holly, then it is my fault. Let me make some calls."

Suddenly, there was a knock on the door. Vance got up to answer it, and I heard a woman's voice say, "Excuse me, I'm looking for Angelica Blackwell. I was told she might be here."

Vance opened the door, and a woman walked in. She was tall and thin, with long, curly blonde hair and bright blue eyes. I recognized her as Elizabeth Connor. I liked to tease Aunt Thelma about using too many beauty potions and creams, but this woman didn't look a day over forty when I knew she was the same age as my aunt.

"Hi, Elizabeth," I said, standing to greet her.

"Diane mentioned that you were trying to track down the person who brought the cursed gift to the party last night. I thought I might be able to help." Elizabeth looked down at Aunt Thelma. The woman had tears in her eyes. "I hate seeing her like this."

I wasn't sure how genuine Elizabeth's crocodile tears were, but I agreed with her.

"What do you know?" Frederick asked, standing up from the corner.

"Oh, hello, Frederick. I didn't see you there." Elizabeth fluffed her hair. "Anyway, as I was saying, I brought a gift to the party, too. It was a bottle of champagne. I didn't see anyone with a gift wrapped in dark blue paper, but I did notice Thelma's ex-husband, Robert, acting strange.

"Who's this again?" Frederick asked, seeming intrigued. I remembered seeing Frederick and my former uncle talking. I wondered if he knew who he was and that the two had been married.

"My former uncle Robert. You talked with him.

Green fitted coat. Tan pants. Aunt Thelma joined your conversation," I supplied. Frederick silently motioned that he understood whom I meant. "Go on," I said to Elizabeth.

"Well, he was hovering near Aunt Thelma most of the night. I thought it was a bit odd, considering he usually keeps to himself, but he was following her around like a puppy dog. Didn't you notice?" Elizabeth said to Frederick.

He shook his head and looked back at Aunt Thelma, not meeting our eyes.

"Anyway, when it was time to open gifts, he suddenly disappeared. Don't you remember?" Elizabeth asked.

"I remember announcing we were going to open gifts, but it never happened," I replied.

"Exactly. You made the announcement, and he practically ran out of the room! And knowing your former uncle, I'm sure he bought her something fabulous. He always had exquisite taste."

Elizabeth made a good point.

"Did we see a gift from Uncle Robert?" I asked Vance.

"Not that I remember, but there's still a lot left unopened at her apartment," Vance answered.

"If I were you, I'd have a talk with him, pronto!" Elizabeth nodded knowingly.

"Thanks, we will." If he hadn't already been on the list of suspects, he would be now.

"We'll make sure to speak with him as soon as possible," Vance added.

"Good luck," she said, giving me a pat on the arm. "Let me know if there's anything else I can do." Elizabeth gave one last look at Aunt Thelma and left the room.

"This Uncle Robert of yours—" Frederick started to say.

"We already planned on talking with him," I interrupted.

"Was he still close with Thelma?" Frederick continued. I noticed a tinge of jealousy in Frederick's voice.

"No, not that I'm aware of. Last night was the first time I'd seen him in years," I answered truthfully.

"Hmmm," Frederick nodded, lost in his thoughts.

I turned to Vance. "I think we should go back to the inn. Remember, Clemmie took notes from the gifts."

"Let's catalog what we have," Vance followed my train of thought.

"And find out what gift Uncle Robert brought," I nodded.

"I'll stay here," Frederick said with determination in his voice.

"You've already been here all day. Do you want me to see if Clemmie can come up and sit with her for a while?" I offered.

"I'll just worry about her if I'm not here," Frederick said, his eyes never leaving Aunt Thelma.

"Okay," I said, understanding his concern. "I'll call you if we figure out anything."

"JELLY! Where have you been? I've been worried sick. No phone call. No messages. You're killing me here!" Percy the Poltergeist wailed.

"How's Thelma doing?" his much calmer ghostly wife, Eleanor, asked.

"She's doing a little better," I replied, grateful for Percy's dramatics. It was always a relief to have a bit of levity in a serious situation.

"That's good to hear," Eleanor said. "But Percy's right. You should have called. We were all worried."

"I know, I'm sorry. It's been a hectic day," I apologized.

"It was here too! The phone's been ringing off the hook. Everyone wants to know how Thelma's doing. But don't you worry, I told them all to get lost!" Percy hooked his thumb over his translucent shoulder.

"He was a bit more polite than that," Eleanor amended.

I doubted that, but I smiled, nonetheless.

"Everything else go okay around here?" I asked.

"For the most part. We heard a bit of a scuffle on the second floor," Eleanor explained.

"A downright fight!" Percy jumped back in the conversation, complete with kung fu hands.

"What happened?" Vance asked.

"Dunno. Eleanor and I floated up there as soon as we heard it, but it was over as soon as it started."

"It's been quiet ever since," Eleanor added.

"I suppose that's good." It would've been better if it hadn't happened at all, but at least it seemed resolved. "Do you mind continuing to cover the inn? Misty was going to stop by," I let my words trail off.

"Oh, she did. We sent her on her way after the last reservation checked in. No sense in having three people on duty."

"Don't you worry. We've got everything covered," Percy replied with a commanding nod.

"If you're sure. Vance and I are tracking some leads. We'd like to work up in the apartment for a little bit."

"Don't let us stop you," Percy shooed us away.

"Did you two eat?" Eleanor looked at us with concern.

"No, not since earlier," I admitted. I'd been too stressed to think about eating.

"Leave it to me then. I'll send something up," Eleanor replied.

"Thanks, that would be great," Vance said.

We turned and walked away, but not before Percy suddenly popped up between us.

"Oh!" I jumped back. I hated when he did that.

Percy thought nothing of it. "One more thing," he lowered his voice even though the lobby was empty. "I thought of someone else. A suspect." Percy raised his eyebrows.

"Who?" I asked.

"Ryan Nante. He used to work here. Your aunt gave him the old heave-ho when she caught him stealing from the office. He's had an attitude ever since."

"Ryan Nante," I repeated the name. He didn't sound familiar.

"It was before your time," Percy said, reading my expression.

"Let me guess, when I lived in Chicago?" I surmised.

"It's not my fault you were there *forever*," Percy rolled his eyes. "But you better look into him. He's a bad dude."

"Okay, we will." But it was going to have to be in the morning. Nighttime had fallen. We needed to head upstairs and do some research before picking back up with the interviews tomorrow.

As we climbed the stairs to Aunt Thelma's apartment, I couldn't shake the feeling of dread that had been following me all day. The thought of Aunt Thelma lying in that hospital bed, cursed and helpless, made my heart ache. But I couldn't let my emotions cloud my judgment. Vance and I needed to figure out who was to blame and make sure they were arrested before they could strike again.

Once we reached the apartment, we set to work cataloging the gifts. Clemmie had done an excellent job of taking notes, and we were able to quickly determine which gifts had come from whom. But when it came to Uncle Robert's gift, there was nothing.

"That's not like him," I confessed while biting into my meatball sandwich. Eleanor had brought up a couple of cokes and bags of chips to go with the subs while we sorted the gifts. "I thought for sure we'd find something extravagant from him."

"Maybe he gave it to her personally at the party," Vance suggested.

"Or maybe the necklace is from him, and Roger is right."

"If he can't have her, no one else can?"

"Exactly."

Vance frowned. "I don't like the sound of that."

"Neither do I," I agreed. "We need to talk to him as soon as possible."

"Do you want to go see him now?" Vance asked.

"I don't even know where he's staying. Let me text the group and see if they know."

"All right," Vance said, finishing his sandwich. "What's our plan for tomorrow?"

"Hopefully, we can interview Uncle Robert and that ex-employee Percy told us about."

"Ryan Nante. I can look into him when we get home."

I looked at my phone. "We should probably head there and feed Rocky." Vance had installed an oversized doggy door for our pet gargoyle so he could come and go as he pleased, but he still looked to us for food and companionship.

"You're right, we should," Vance said, standing up. "Let's head home. You need to get some rest, too." I wanted to protest, but Vance was right. I'd spent most of the day running on pure adrenaline, and I was dead on my feet.

We locked up the apartment and made our way downstairs. Despite the exhaustion that weighed heavily on my shoulders, I couldn't shake off the feeling of unease that had been gnawing at me all day. There were too many suspects, too many possibilities, and not enough evidence. I knew it was going to be a long road ahead of us, but I was determined to get to the bottom of it, no matter what it took.

With that in mind, we made our way back to our house. Vance got to work researching Ryan Nante while I tried to settle in for the night. I filled the clawfoot tub with hot water and poured in one of Connie's calming tonics from the potion shop. Swirls of purple and pink mixed into the water, releasing the soothing smell of lavender and eucalyptus.

Minutes after sinking into the water, Vance's voice came through the bathroom door.

"Ryan has a criminal record," Vance's voice was muffled, but I could still make out his words. "Multiple arrests for assault and battery."

"When was the most recent one?"

"Couple months ago. He was caught shoplifting in Savannah. Oh, here's another one... I can't believe this." Vance's voice was filled with disgust.

"What?"

"He stole the donation jar from the hospital's gift shop."

"He did not!" How awful.

But Vance wasn't done. "There's more. I see multiple arrests for assault and battery. Domestic disputes with his mother. He uses magic for all the wrong reasons."

"He's a witch, then."

"I'd say a warlock at this point." Warlocks were witches who'd switched over to the dark side, so to speak. "The list goes on. I'll print it out."

"Okay, thanks."

By the time I got out of the bath, Vance had looked into other aspects of Ryan's life as well. He knew who his friends were, where he liked to spend time, and what kind of activities he engaged in on a regular basis. We learned that he was quite popular in Oak Creek, a nearby town, often seen out with different people at various bars and clubs. He seemed to have made a lot of connections over the years—some good ones, others questionable—but none of them seemed directly connected to this case. Regardless, Vance and I knew that we needed to talk to him in person.

Chapter 7

The next morning, we woke up early and headed over to the inn. Aunt Thelma always did the bank deposit on Monday morning, and I didn't want to skip it. We'd worked hard over the last two years to get the inn updated and turning a profit, I didn't want things sliding south just because she was incapacitated for a day or two. I refused to think it would take any longer for us to catch the culprit and break the curse.

I called Frederick before leaving the house. Aunt Thelma was still the same. He didn't see any changes in her condition, which was both a relief and a disappointment. I was hoping that the curse would lift itself, but it seemed like Charity had been right, and only the culprit could break the spell. I promised Frederick I'd stop up there before lunchtime and wouldn't hang up until he promised he'd get something to eat.

"You know he's not going to leave," Vance replied after hearing our conversation.

"I know, which is sweet and heartbreaking." I hadn't realized how much Frederick loved Aunt Thelma until he moved into town. I knew the two were smitten with one another, but their emotions went deeper than that. It was nice to see after Aunt Thelma had been unlucky with love for so many years.

"I'll call my mom and see if she can drop some food off at the hospital," Vance offered.

"That's a great idea."

While Vance drove, I checked in with the rest of our friends. Clemmie and Diane said Elizabeth thought nothing of crashing Aunt Thelma's party. She claimed she didn't know it was an invitation-only event. I replied that Elizabeth stopped by the hospital yesterday and pointed the finger at Uncle Robert. Misty offered to come with me to interview him, but I asked if she could lend a hand at the inn instead. Percy was doing a fine job now, but you never knew when he was going to pitch a temper tantrum. Clemmie and Diane said they were heading up to the hospital this morning, and they'd make sure Frederick ate Heather's food.

I put down my phone and gazed out the car window. The morning sun cast a warm golden glow over the village. A hint of magic could be seen in the air, tiny glimmers of stardust that glowed against the sun-kissed sky. It was a gentle reminder that I was a smart, powerful witch. I'd solved plenty of other cases, and I'd solve this one too.

As we stepped inside the inn, the smell of freshly brewed coffee and warm cinnamon rolls filled the air, making my stomach growl with hunger.

"Good morning," Percy called out from the front desk. "Eleanor has breakfast waiting for you in the kitchen."

"How'd you know we were stopping by?"

"Because it's Monday, and you need to do the bank deposit." Percy tapped his temple as if he was proud of himself for remembering such a detail.

"Sometimes you're smarter than I give you credit for," I joked with the poltergeist.

He replied by blowing me a raspberry.

"Love you too," I called back as we passed through the lobby.

"Morning, Angelica," Clemmie's date, Theo, said as we passed by. He had a newspaper tucked under his arm with a cup of coffee in hand.

"Good morning," I said with a wave. I wondered if Clemmie had told Theo about Carl being in town. If I remembered correctly, Theo would be checking out tomorrow. His reservation had been for a long weekend. I shook my head. For not the first time, I was glad I only had one man in my life, and we were now happily married.

Inside the cozy kitchenette, Eleanor had set out a plate of cinnamon rolls. "Diane made them. I just slipped them in the oven to keep them warm," she explained while pouring us each a cup of coffee and sitting down with us at the table.

"How did you sleep, Angelica?" she asked, looking at me with concern.

"Not great," I admitted. "I keep thinking about Aunt Thelma."

"I know, dear," Eleanor said, patting my hand. "But you have to remember Thelma wouldn't want you to be consumed with worry. She would want you to use your abilities to solve the case."

"Trust me, I know." I took a sip of my coffee and tried to keep my emotions from getting the best of me.

As we finished breakfast and I gathered the bank deposit, I received a call from Libby.

"Hey, I'm still going through the footage, but there's someone who looks suspicious. I'm going to text you a clip. Let me know if he looks familiar to you."

It didn't take long for the clip to be downloaded on my phone, and once we hit play, I knew why she had sent it. The man in the video wore catering staff attire, but his tray was always empty. He was skulking around the party crowd, hovering near different groups while they talked. They were oblivious to him as he moved through the guests. "Did he just steal that man's wallet?" I said into my phone while the video played.

"That's what I thought too. Do you know him?" Libby asked.

"No, I don't. Hey Vance?" I said to my husband, who was helping Eleanor clean up the kitchenette. "Can you come here and look at this? Libby's on speaker. She found this guy on the surveillance video." I restarted the footage and angled my phone so Vance could watch it.

Vince took a close look. "That's Ryan Nante."

"Are you kidding me?" I replied.

"Who's Ryan Dante?" Libby asked.

"He's one of our suspects. I've never met him before. He used to work at the inn," I explained.

"I'm positive that's him. I'd bet money on it. I saw about twenty photos of him when I looked him up last night," Vance confirmed.

"Thank you so much for the video. This is super helpful," I told Libby.

"You're welcome. I'll keep looking and let you know if I see him do anything else."

"Okay, thank you. I appreciate it." I turned to Vance. "What do you think? Should we track down Ryan first?"

"I think that's a good idea."

Given Ryan's tendency to hit up the bars and

the nightlife in Oak Creek, it would've been easier to find him if it would've been a Friday night. But seeing it was a Monday morning, it was going to be a little bit trickier.

"I don't have a current address, but I know who his probation officer is," Vance said. Probation officers weren't a thing in Silverlake like they were in the mortal world.

"That's a start. Where are they at?" I hoped it wasn't too far away.

"Where else, but Oak Creek," Vance confirmed.

"At least he's consistent. I guess let's give the officer a call and see what we can find out." Seeing the probation officer was most likely a mortal, we wouldn't be able to explain the cursed necklace, but we could show him the potential pickpocketing video.

I waited while Vance placed the call, but he didn't seem to be getting anywhere.

"No one's answering. Want to take a drive?"

"Yeah, let's do that."

Forty-five minutes later, after making the bank deposit and driving to Oak Creek, we stepped into the fluorescent-lit lobby of the federal office. The woman behind the front desk smiled warmly, if only briefly, as her attention was pulled in numerous directions.

"Karen?" A lady's voice called out from the back, "do you know why the copier isn't working?"

"Sorry, one minute, please," the receptionist said to us as she power walked toward the woman's voice to answer her question. The phone rang at her desk at the same time, but there was no one else to answer it.

"Sorry about that," she apologized a minute later, returning to her desk.

"Karen?" Another person, this time a man, called out from his office, "Did I get a call from Judge Ford yet?"

"No, Frank, you didn't," the receptionist called over her shoulder before turning and shaking her head at us. "Sorry about that, we're a bit short staffed. What can I do for you?"

"We're looking for a Mr. Johnson. I believe he's Ryan Nante's probation officer," Vance explained.

"You that bounty hunter?" the receptionist asked.

"What?" I looked at Vance.

"Never mind. I'll get Mr. Johnson for you." The phone rang before she could say anything else.

"Bounty hunter?" I repeated to Vance as we took a seat in the blue plastic chairs that lined the wall. "Does that mean they don't know where Ryan is?"

"Guess we're going to find out."

A few minutes later, a deep voice called out from the back office. "Greetings." We turned to see a tall, middle-aged man with graying hair and glasses. "I'm Mr. Johnson. Come on back."

The office cubicles were arranged in neat rows, with plain fabric dividers and muted colors in the decor. We walked down an aisle until we came to the last one in the back. Mr. Johnson ushered us in and offered us a seat. "I understand you're here to talk about Mr. Nante. How can I help?"

"We're hoping you can tell us where he is," Vance started by saying.

I took out my phone and brought up the video. "We had a party for my aunt this past weekend, and we think he might have pickpocketed a few wallets. We'd like to talk with him."

Mr. Johnson watched the video. "Don't you think this is something you should take to the police?"

"I'm sorry, I should have introduced myself. I'm Deputy Blackwell, and this is my husband, Vance Blackwell. He's a defense attorney." I didn't think I wanted to be a deputy when Sheriff Reynolds first deputized me, but I had to admit, the title came in handy a time or two.

"I see then. Well, I can tell you this doesn't surprise me. Ryan's been on probation for the last six months for drug possession," Mr. Johnson said. "He'd been doing well in his program, but we've had a hard time getting a hold of him lately. He missed his last check-in appointment, and I haven't been able to reach him since."

"Do you have any idea where he might be?" Vance asked.

"I don't, which is why we've outsourced it," Mr. Johnson replied.

"The bounty hunter," I surmised.

"We don't usually jump on everyone who violates parole, but Mr. Nante is wanted in connection with other crimes. Grand larceny, last I heard," Mr. Johnson added before we could ask. "Let me give you the DA's name working the case." The parole officer scribbled a name and number on his notepad and tore off the paper. "He should be able to give you the latest."

"Thanks. We appreciate it." I took the paper and tucked it into my pocket.

"Do you want to give him a call?" I asked Vance once we were outside. Lawyers seemed to have their own jargon, and I thought Vance could get further than I could. I squinted into the sun and looked down the sidewalk. Oak Creek's main street was lined with trendy shops and restaurants, bustling with people going to and fro.

"Sure, I'll make the call."

While Vance talked to the DA, I wished there was a spell I could use to trace Ryan. It was too bad you had to love a person in order for tracking spells to work.

"Well, the DA said he has a few leads, but Ryan hasn't turned up yet. He'll call us when he does," Vance said after hanging up.

"You researched Ryan. Does he have any family in the area?"

"Yeah, his mom, but he's not hiding out there. The police have already checked."

"No, it's not that. What about a spell? You know he has magic in his blood. Do you think his mom would try a tracking spell?"

"And turn in her own son?" Vance looked skeptical.

"Maybe?"

Vance seemed to weigh my words, and then a light bulb went off. I swear, I could see his eyes light up. "No, but you know who might?"

"Who?"

"His ex-girlfriend. She filed recent charges," Vance looked around the street. "I need my computer. I don't know why I didn't think of this." I followed Vance back to the truck while he filled me in. "Her name is Lila. I can't remember her last name. Ryan lived with her in between stints at the county jail. I'm not sure if she loves him or if she ever did, but it's worth a shot."

Chapter 8

We drove back to Silverlake and parked outside our cozy home. Vance went straight to his computer while I brewed some tea. The idea of using a tracking spell was clever, but I couldn't shake off the feeling that something was off. Maybe it was my intuition as a witch, or maybe it was just my nerves getting the best of me.

While Vance continued to research, I cleaned the house. I couldn't sit still while Aunt Thelma's attacker was still out there. I moved quickly around the rooms, dusting the tables, sweeping the floors, and scrubbing the counters while Rocky pranced after me, picking up on my nervous energy.

"It's okay, boy. We'll get Aunt Thelma back to normal soon," I said for my benefit more than his. I was determined to make the house spotless while mentally calculating our next move and sipping tea in the process.

I was about to head out and interview my former uncle on my own when Vance interrupted. "Got it!" he exclaimed, breaking me out of my thoughts. "Her name is Lila Monroe. Lives right in town in the apartments next to the high school."

"Okay, how do you think we should approach her? We can't just show up at her doorstep and ask her to track her ex for us, can we?"

"Why not? She filed charges against him. Child support charges. She probably wants to find him."

"Or she wants nothing to do with him. I feel like it can go either way."

"You're right, which is why we'll have to play it by ear and see how it goes."

I agreed with Vance. As much as I liked having a plan, this time, we'd have to make it up as we went along.

"Daniel also emailed me," Vance said, laptop in tow. "He looked into Mr. Ansel some more. We might want to interview him again."

"Why, what does he say?"

"He said the businessman made some poor investments and engaged in bad business practices that cost him thousands of dollars over the years. Mr. Ansel tried to recoup his losses with some questionable ventures, but they only put him further in the hole."

"Which was why he wanted to partner with Aunt Thelma?"

"It seems like he was desperate for money. He probably saw the inn as his last chance to turn things around."

"I wonder if there's any connection between Ryan and Mr. Ansel?"

"I'll have Daniel look." Vance put the computer down and took out his phone, presumably to text Daniel.

"If Mr. Ansel was involved, what do you think the motive is? Revenge?"

"It's possible. Maybe he blames your aunt for his financial ruin?"

"Okay, let me know what Daniel discovers. In the meantime, I think we should check in with Lila about Ryan and then interview my uncle. We need to start eliminating suspects." So far, it seemed like we were spinning in circles.

"Let's head to Lila's, and then we'll go from there."

"It's a plan." I gave Rocky an oversized bone to keep him busy, and then we locked up and headed out.

THE APARTMENT COMPLEX was broken into three main separate buildings, each one three stories tall. A community pool and playground took up the courtyard between them. Vance and I walked toward the building where Lila's apartment was located and went inside, climbing the stairs to the second floor. Vance knocked on the door, and we waited. After a few moments, the door creaked open, and a young woman with long, curly hair stood in front of us.

"Can I help you?" Her voice was soft but guarded.

"I'm Vance, and this is my wife, Angelica. We're looking for Ryan Nante. We heard that you might be able to help us find him," Vance explained.

Lila's eyes widened, and she stepped back as if she wanted to close the door. "I haven't heard from Ryan in weeks." A baby began to cry in the background. The young woman closed her eyes. "Why won't he take a nap," she pleaded in desperation.

"Do you want a hand?" I offered. "I can try and settle the baby, and maybe you can help us try and find Ryan?"

"Why, what do you want with him?" The woman looked leery.

"We want to talk with him. My aunt was recently cursed after her birthday party, and he was there."

"Who's your aunt?"

"Thelma Nightingale."

Lila made a circle with her mouth as if she was saying, *Ohhhhh*. "Yeah, Ryan doesn't like her."

"Which is why I need to talk with him. Give him a chance to explain himself." I left out the part about pickpocketing.

I thought Lila was going to say sorry and shut the door, but the baby's wails in the background broke her resolve. "Sure, fine. Come on in."

We followed Lila into her small and cramped apartment. The living room was filled with baby toys, and there was a faint smell of baby powder in the air. Lila picked up the crying baby and rocked him gently.

"He's teething," she explained. "He's been crying all day."

"May I?" I asked, outstretching my arms.

"Be my guest." Lila handed her son over. I'd guess he was no more than six months old. "I had a teething potion, but it ran out." Lila looked around the room. She didn't have to finish the sentence for us to pick up the meaning. Lila didn't have the money to buy more.

I shushed the little guy and bounced him against my hip, hoping to calm him down. He fussed for a bit as he mouthed his fist.

"I'm sorry if I seem hesitant to help, but Ryan and I didn't end things on the best terms."

"That's understandable," I said, trying to ease her worries.

"I haven't heard from him in weeks," Lila repeated, her eyes filled with pain. "He hasn't even checked in on his son."

Vance leaned forward and patted the baby on the back. "Do you have any idea where he might be?" Vance kept his voice soothing.

Lila sighed, and the baby's cries slowly began to quiet down. "Last I heard, he was staying at a motel outside of Oak Creek. But that was a few weeks ago. I haven't heard anything since."

"Have you tried a tracing spell?" I suggested.

"Why? He doesn't want to be here. I decided a long time ago that I wasn't going to force him to. Giving him my heart was the biggest mistake of my life."

"Would you be willing to try? If Ryan cursed my aunt, he's the only one who can break it." I started bouncing the baby once more, getting him to drift off to sleep.

The color drained from Lila's face. "I'd like to say Ryan would never do that, but he..." Lila visibly swallowed. "He really doesn't like your aunt."

"I know."

Lila's eyes flickered with a mix of emotions. Vance and I exchanged a knowing look. "I'll do the tracking spell," Lila said finally, her voice barely above a whisper. "But I can't guarantee that it will work."

"We just want you to try," Vance replied.

Lila nodded. "Do you mind holding him for a minute longer?"

"No, not at all." I patted the baby's back. He snoozed soundly against my shoulder, his drool seeping through my shirt.

Lila got up and retrieved a few supplies from around the room. She grabbed her wand, two small candles, and a family picture that included Ryan. After lighting the candles, she placed them in the center of the living room and knelt beside them. Taking a deep breath, Lila said the incantation to search for Ryan: Éla edó Diafotízo.

A sudden gust of wind blew through the room, causing the candles to flicker wildly. The temperature dropped, and I shivered, feeling a chill run down my spine. I held the baby tightly to my chest to keep him warm. The wind grew stronger, and the objects in the room began to rattle and shake. Despite my best efforts, the baby started to fuss once more, his cries adding to the chaos. Lila's eyes were closed in concentration, her lips moving silently as she focused on the spell. Suddenly, there was a bright flash of light, and the wind died down. The candles went out, and the room was plunged into darkness.

For a moment, there was silence, and then the lights flickered back on, one by one. Lila slowly opened her eyes and looked around the room. "I can feel him," she whispered. "He's nearby." At that moment, the front door burst open, and Ryan walked in. "What's going on here?" he demanded, looking around at the chaotic scene before him.

"That was fast," I mumbled sarcastically to Vance before shushing the baby. Spells could be powerful, but they couldn't summon Ryan home that fast. He must have already been on his way.

"We were looking for you," Lila explained, standing.

"I see that. What the heck is going on? Who are you, and why are you holding my son," Ryan glared at me.

"Oh, like you care now," Lila shot back. "I should kick you out, and I would, but I really want to hear what excuse you'll come up with for cursing her aunt."

"Who's your aunt?" Ryan asked.

"Thelma Nightingale."

Ryan's expression was filled with joy. "Is she dead? Tell me she's dead," he smiled and tossed his coat on the nearby chair. I couldn't believe what I was hearing. Ryan's cruel and callous words made my blood boil. "I can't believe I didn't think of that. It wasn't me, but when you find out who it was, let me know so I can send them a thank you card!" He smiled broadly.

I handed the baby back to Lila and stepped

forward, my wand out and ready to use if needed. I liked to think of myself as being levelheaded, but all bets were off the table when you insulted those I loved.

"How dare you!" I snapped at Ryan. "Thelma Nightingale is a kind and beloved member of our community. She does not deserve your disrespect."

Ryan sneered at me. "I don't care about your community or your aunt. And I certainly don't care about you."

Vance stepped forward, putting himself between me and Ryan. "That's enough, I'm calling the sheriff."

"Go ahead and do that, and I'll tell him you're trespassing on my property," Ryan snarled.

"You don't live here," Lila shot back. "Not anymore."

"Fine. I'm leaving." Ryan grabbed his coat and threw some money at Lila. "That's for the kid," he said sarcastically before turning back to us. "Don't follow me."

Unfortunately for Ryan, I didn't listen. He might not have cursed Aunt Thelma, but he was still wanted for questioning by the Oak Creek police department, not to mention violating parole.

Before he could make it out the door, I pointed my wand at his back and shouted, "Glacio!" A stream of blue light burst from the tip of my wand

and hit him squarely in the back, causing him to freeze in place.

I wasn't sure how Lila would react. I knew she was angry with Ryan, but she had loved him at one time, and he was the father of her son. But when she shouted, "Bravo!" and laughed with her son on her hip, I knew everything would be okay.

Chapter 9

Vance and I didn't leave right away. Not before Sheriff Reynolds arrived and arrested Ryan for violating parole and making sure Lila was okay, and her son, whose name turned out to be Sebastian, was settled back down.

"I wish Ryan was our guy," I told Vance after buckling my seatbelt. "I'd love nothing more than to make that slimeball pay."

"I'm sorry he said those awful things about Aunt Thelma."

"I know, but it's not just about what he said. It's about how he treats people in general. The fact that he's willing to walk away from his son like that?" My voice was laced with anger. "Ryan's a cruel and heartless person."

Vance nodded in agreement and turned the

engine over. "But now we need to find the real culprit and make them break the curse."

"You're right." I smiled at Vance. "Thanks for always having my back."

"Always." He reached over and took my hand. "Now, where is your uncle Robert staying?"

I took my cell phone out. Diane and Roger were looking into it. I read through the string of text messages. "Clemmie says Aunt Thelma's still resting comfortably," I offered while looking for a message from Diane.

"I suppose that's the best we can hope for."

"Oh, here we go. Uncle Robert is fixing up a small cabin on the outskirts of the forest. Diane sent me the address." I showed Vance the message.

"Alright, let's go pay him a visit," Vance said, turning the car towards the lake.

When we finally arrived at the cabin, Uncle Robert was outside. He had planks of cedar propped up against the cabin, with one resting between two sawhorses. The cabin's old shutters were piled off to the side.

Uncle Robert was wearing a pair of jeans with a flannel shirt and a straw hat. He had on a tool belt filled with all sorts of tools and looked like he had been working hard all morning. As we got closer, I noticed the surprise in his eyes as he saw us.

"My goodness, what brings you two out here?" He wiped his hands on his jeans and stepped forward to give me a hug like old times. The move caught me entirely by surprise. I hugged him back on reflex. "Sorry I didn't get a chance to talk with you at the party. Work called," he replied as if that explained it all.

"Work?" I motioned to the cabin.

"Not this old place. Chief Brody needed backup. Transfiguration spell gone wrong. Loretta Johnson's tail is gone, but she still has the whiskers." Uncle Robert smiled.

"Loretta Johnson tried to transform into a cat?" I asked. I didn't know Loretta had it in her. I could transform into a feline, my alter ego named Penelope, but it was a gift passed down from my mother, and even then, I needed my magical pendant to pull it off. My fingers reached for my tiger eye necklace out of habit.

"And climb a tree. Hence the fire department," Uncle Robert pointed to his chest. "I'm just happy Chief let me rejoin the force after being gone all these years. Anyway, enough about that. What can I do for you two? Do you want a tour?" Uncle Robert motioned to the cabin.

I looked at Vance. It was clear Uncle Robert had no idea Aunt Thelma had been cursed.

"We're actually here to talk about Thelma," Vance said, his tone serious.

Uncle Robert looked taken back. "What's going on with Thelma? Is she okay?"

"Not really. She's been cursed," I said, stepping forward.

Uncle Robert's eyes widened. "Cursed? I can't believe it. Who would do such a thing? Is it that new boyfriend of hers? I told Thelma he gave me a weird vibe."

"Frederick?" I asked.

"That's him. I don't trust him. Not one bit!" Uncle Robert began to pace, "Is she okay? Can you reverse it? Where's Constantine? Wait, she doesn't live in town anymore, does she? What's that young healer's name? I met her last week at the bakery."

"Charity," I supplied. "She's working on it, but we need to find out who cursed her."

"I already told you; look into Frederick."

I didn't have the heart to tell my uncle that Frederick loved Aunt Thelma. There's no way he was to blame. Uncle Robert wouldn't believe me anyway.

"What else can I do? Can I see her? Where is she?" Uncle Robert fired off his questions without waiting for an answer. He unclipped his tool belt and patted his pockets as if looking for his car keys.

"She's at the hospital, but I don't think it's a good idea," Vance said.

"Frederick's there. I'm not sure how much Aunt Thelma can hear. I don't want to upset her," I explained.

"You left her with Frederick?!" Uncle Robert roared.

"You have to trust me. He didn't do this," I tried to reason with my former uncle even though I just said I wasn't going to.

"Oh, baloney!"

"I trust him. Vance trusts him. He's a good guy," I explained. As for the rest of Mount Holly, I couldn't be too sure. Mr. Frederick hadn't gotten back to me regarding his potential enemies.

"What's trust but something to be broken," Uncle Robert replied dryly.

"How about this? She loves him. He loves her. I know that's not what you want to hear, but it's the truth. If you really wanted to help my aunt, you'd quit acting jealous and help us figure out who really is to blame."

Uncle Robert's face fell at my words. I could see the hurt and disbelief etched on his face as he tried to process the news of his ex-wife's new love. He ran a hand through his hair and let out a deep sigh. It was clear that he was struggling to come to terms with the fact that Aunt Thelma had moved on. As much as he might have denied it, I'd bet any amount of money that a part of him still harbored hope they might reconcile someday. But now, that hope had been shattered, and he looked more defeated than I'd ever seen him. "She really loves that guy?"

"The two of you were a lifetime ago," I reminded Uncle Robert.

"I just thought ... never mind, it doesn't matter what I thought. I'd still like to see her." Uncle Robert put his hands up in surrender. "I won't start anything, I promise. I don't think you should've written Frederick off that quickly, but I won't say anything."

"Let me call Frederick and see how she's doing first," and give him a heads up that my former uncle would stop in. I know Uncle Robert said he wouldn't start something, but I couldn't be sure Frederick wouldn't goad him into an argument. People tended to do strange things when they were stressed out and in love with the same woman.

While I was on the phone with Frederick, Vance got a call from Daniel. He'd been looking into Mr. Ansel some more at Vance's request. Uncle Robert didn't wait to hear what Frederick or Daniel said. He hopped in his truck and left while we were still on our phones.

"Daniel says Mr. Ansel is broke," Vance said after hanging up.

"Come again?"

"He's in debt worse than we realized. Daniel didn't find any connection to Ryan, not that we expect him to anymore, but there are plenty of creditors after him."

"And that adds weight that he might have cursed her for revenge."

"What gift did he give her again?" Vance asked.

I twisted my lips in thought. "A bottle of champagne. Salon Le Mes something or another. It had a big S on the bottle."

"Salon Le Mesnil Blanc de Blancs?" Vance questioned.

"Yes?" I pulled up my phone and tried to spell it out. Thankfully, the internet pointed me in the right direction. I recognized a picture of the champagne bottle. Vance had been right. "Yes, that's the one." Then I saw the price tag. "Holy guacamole. He gave her a two-thousand-dollar bottle of champagne? He can't be *that* broke."

"Unless he took it out of his private collection," Vance countered.

"Or maybe stole it." Witches conjured things all the time. Of course, if you did it without paying, it was called stealing. Unfortunately, a mortal (AKA nonmagical person) would never know what'd happened.

"Let's back up. We have someone who doesn't have much money still giving lavish gifts," Vance said.

"Right. I think it could go two ways. Maybe Mr. Ansel was trying to get back on Aunt Thelma's good graces to broker a business deal."

"Because he needs the money," Vance nodded.

"Or the expensive gift was to throw us off."

"If he can get his hands on expensive champagne, I assume he can get his hands on a pricey necklace."

"That's a good point. I wonder if there's a way to trace the necklace's origin. I doubt they bought it in town."

"We could still ask Katie at Splendid Gems. Maybe it's a known designer or something?" Vance suggested.

"If we had a picture of it, we could try and do a reverse image search online too."

"That's another good idea."

"I can call Charity and see if she still has it or where it's at." Maybe we could stop by and snap a picture.

Chapter 10

My brilliant plan didn't initially seem to get us too far. While Charity still had the necklace in her possession and was able to take a picture and text it to me, the internet couldn't match it to anything online.

Our next step was to visit Katie.

Splendid Gems was a small, quaint shop with a glass window that glinted in the sunlight, show-casing intricate pieces of jewelry. Inside the shop, there were cases full of tempting baubles and gems, their sparkling facades beckoning customers inside.

"Is that Daniel?" I pointed to a man walking out of the jewelry store. His back was to us, walking in the opposite direction.

Vance followed my direction. "I think so."

"I wonder if he knows."

"Knows what?"

"That Misty's been thinking about getting married."

"Want me to find out?" Vance jokingly moved as if he was going to call out to our friend.

"Don't you dare," I tugged Vance's arm toward the front door and away from the sidewalk. "Misty would kill me. What if he has no clue and is looking at new cufflinks or something?"

Vance opened the door, and we stepped inside.

"Hey, you two, how are you doing? Everything okay with your ring?" Katie asked.

I looked down at my sparkling wedding ring. "No, it's great. We had a question about a case we're working. I'm not sure if you heard, but Aunt Thelma was cursed."

"What? No! I hadn't heard. I've been working nonstop. What happened?"

"It was a necklace," Vance explained.

I took out my phone and opened the text app to bring up the picture. "I know it's a long shot, but does this look familiar?"

Katie's eyes lit up. "Oh, my goodness. Yes, it does. I customized that necklace for an older gentleman a couple of days ago."

My jaw dropped open as I looked at Vance with a shocked expression. Finally, a break in the case.

"Do you know who he was?" Vance asked.

"No. I didn't recognize him. Definitely not a local.

Let me think. He paid in cash." Katie tapped her chin. "He came in here asking about the necklace and wanted to know if it could be made with diamonds instead of sapphires." She paused and looked away as if something had just clicked in her mind. "Actually, now that I think about it, he mentioned something about a special occasion that needed to be celebrated."

"Did he say what occasion it was?" I asked, trying to keep my voice steady.

Katie shook her head. "No, he didn't mention anything specific. But he seemed very excited about it."

"Do you know Ivan Ansel?" Vance asked.

"Who?"

I searched for his picture online and was thankful when a relatively recent one turned up. "This guy."

Katie leaned in to get a better look. "I've seen him around town lately, but no, that's not him."

"Are you sure?" Vance asked.

"He's about the same age, but this man had darker skin and wire-rimmed glasses. He was very polite. Charming even."

That didn't narrow it down much.

Katie looked apologetic. "I wish I could be more helpful."

"No, that's okay. You have been helpful." While we knew Mr. Ansel hadn't stopped by the jewelry store himself, we couldn't rule out anyone who worked for him.

"What about Elizabeth's husband? She's married, isn't she?" Vance asked.

"Are you talking about Elizabeth Connor?" Katie asked.

"Yes," I answered for Vance.

"It wasn't Donald. He's a regular customer," Katie answered. "Elizabeth loves jewelry, and she's pretty particular."

"Oh." I couldn't keep the disappointment from creeping into my voice.

"Well, there goes that theory," Vance commented.

I turned my attention back to Katie. "If he comes back in, can you try and get his name?"

"I'll do my best," Katie promised.

We thanked Katie, and then we headed out of the store.

As we walked back to the car, I stopped short when a folded piece of paper fluttered from beneath the windshield wiper. Written in bold black ink were the words: **BACK OFF OR ELSE.**

"What is it?" Vance asked.

I handed the paper over for him to read and then turned my attention to our surroundings to see if anyone was watching us, but everything in Village Square looked like business as usual. A few children chased each other around and around the shops while the adults sat on benches and caught up with friends. Elderly couples strolled arm in arm, taking in the pleasant summer afternoon. Dogs were leashed and walked by their owners, tails wagging as they sniffed the flower beds surrounding the sidewalks. Not a single soul looked like they wished anyone harm.

I looked over Vance's shoulder and reread the note. "It looks like we're on the right track. Where to next?"

"You guys okay?" Connie, the potion shop owner, asked from her shop's front door.

"You didn't, by chance, see anyone acting suspicious? Someone just left us a note." My eyes scanned the scene once more.

"What? No, come on in, though." Connie held her shop's door open.

Connie's potion shop was a haven of arcane ingredients and mystical artifacts. The interior was stocked with shelves full of glass jars, each containing a colorful array of liquids, powders, and dried herbs. The fragrant scent of incense filled the air, mingling with the steam that wafted up from the bubbling cauldron that always stood behind the counter.

"I'm working on your aunt's counter curse potion," Connie explained. She added a fine white powder to the pot and began stirring it with a heavy wooden spoon. The smell of peppermint and eucalyptus filled the air, mixing with the musky scent of other unknown ingredients. I looked around the small jars and bottles beside her. Some were labeled with neat, precise handwriting, while others had faded or smudged labels, adding to the mystery of their contents.

"It's a universal antidote. Not sure how effective it will be, but until we know who cursed Thelma, it's the best I can do."

The cauldron emitted a soft, glowing light as the potion started to take shape.

"How long will it take to brew?" I asked, trying to keep my voice steady.

Connie looked up from the cauldron, wiping her forehead with the back of her hand. "It's hard to say. The potion needs time to fully infuse, and we need to be careful with the measurements. One wrong ingredient, and all goes POOF. Whoever cursed the necklace infused it heavily with their magic. It's almost like a signature. I tried to trace it, but it seems to be cloaked."

"In other words, a dark warlock cursed the necklace," Vance said.

"Maybe even a sorcerer," Connie agreed. Sorcerers were one step up on the evil magic scale. I'd dealt with a sorcerer before, or rather a sorcerous. It was an experience I didn't want to repeat.

"We were just at the jewelry shop. Katie remembers an older gentleman who came in with the necklace. She said he didn't seem familiar. He had darker skin and wire-rimmed glasses. Have you seen anyone that might fit that description?"

"You mean besides all of Clemmie's new boyfriends?" Connie shook her head.

"How many are there?" I was almost afraid to ask.

"Last I checked, three. I've seen her stroll by arm in arm with each and every one of them. I don't know how she keeps them straight."

"What? I knew of two but not three." I took the threatening note out of my pocket to show Connie and see what she thought. "This was just what was left on Vance's truck." I opened the note and was shocked to see it was blank. "What in the world?" I flipped the note over. It was like it had been written in invisible ink.

Connie leaned in closer, "That's interesting." She took the piece of paper and examined it closely, her eyes narrowing in concentration. "Hang on, let me see something." Connie took a small, clear dropper bottle from beside the cauldron and care-fully squeezed the rubber bulb with her thumb and forefinger. She pinched the bulb to release the droplets of shimmering blue liquid onto the paper. As the potion soaked in, the ink started to reappear. "This is the same magic used to infuse the neck-lace," Connie said as she continued to study the note. "It's a complex spell, one that requires a lot of power and knowledge. Whoever did this knew what they were doing."

"Is it even worth showing the police?" I asked.

"I'd still tell them about it, but I doubt they'll find any evidence on the note. The spell would've erased everything, like fingerprints."

I refolded the paper and put it back in my pocket.

"I'll head up to the hospital as soon as the potion is ready." She glanced at the cauldron.

"Thank you," I said, grateful for her help.

As Connie continued to work on the potion, Vance and I stood around the shop, trying to come up with a plan. We knew we were missing a crucial piece of information, something that could help us break the curse and catch the person responsible.

"Where do we go from here?" Vance asked, breaking the silence.

"Well, we know the person responsible is still in town," I replied.

"Chances are they've been following us."

"Right. That means that it's not Uncle Robert. Not that I thought it was after we talked to him today."

"It's not Frederick because he's been at the hospital around the clock."

"It could still be Mr. Ansel even though Katie didn't recognize him."

"You mean someone who works for him?"

"Right. It could also be someone who knows Frederick. I think we should check back with him and see if he's thought of anyone we should look into." I should've asked him when I spoke with him earlier, but I'd been distracted when Daniel had called.

Vance thought for a moment, "Maybe we should also check the shops next to the jewelry store and see if anyone else remembers the older man."

"It would help if we had a picture." Katie's description didn't give us much to go by.

As we were still puzzling over the possible motive of the unknown man who had the necklace modified, my phone rang. I glanced at the caller ID and saw that it was the community center. "This is Angelica," I said, answering the call.

"You're not going to believe this," Libby said breathlessly as soon as I picked up. "I was reviewing the security footage from Aunt Thelma's party, and I think I found something."

My heart leaped in my chest. "What did you see?"

"Well, there was this man. I vaguely remember seeing him, but I don't know his name. He came in through the side door about an hour before the party. He's dressed like all the other men; except I think he's carrying the present. The one you told me about."

"Are you kidding me? Can you send me the

footage? We'll take a look and see if I can figure out anything else."

"I have to email it because it's a bit longer."

"That's fine."

I could hear Libby click on her keyboard in the background. "Okay, sent."

"Thank you so much."

"Good luck!" Libby said and hung up.

"Libby thinks she has the person with the gift on camera." I obsessively refreshed my email until I saw the message from Libby pop up.

"What's going on?" Connie asked.

"We might've just caught our bad guy," I explained while waiting for the video to download. The moment it did, I pushed play.

We all huddled around the phone and watched the footage from the community center's security camera. I wasn't sure what I was expecting, maybe a man with a hoodie sneaking around, or someone who clearly looked suspicious. But no, this man marched right in with the gift on display. He wasn't hiding anything.

I gasped when he was close enough to the camera to make out his features. "Theo?"

"Clemmie's boyfriend?" Vance leaned my phone toward him so he could get a closer look.

"That's him, right?"

"Yeah, that's him," Vance confirmed.

"Let me see again," Connie asked.

I tilted the phone her way. Connie nodded. "I've seen him around town with her."

My mind struggled to catch up.

"Why did Theo give your aunt a cursed necklace?" Vance asked.

"We need to talk with him, now!" I was already headed for the door.

Chapter 11

We wasted no time in heading to Mystic Inn to confront Theo about the necklace.

"Jelly? What's going on?" Percy asked as Vance and I marched into the lobby.

"Is Theo still here?" I asked as I came around the registration desk and started typing in the reservation system.

"That gentleman Ms. Clemmie is seeing? That old guy with the glasses?" Percy clarified.

"He wears glasses?" I remembered Katie's comment about our mystery man being an older gentleman who wore glasses.

"He sure does. When reading the paper anyway."

"That's the one, then. He still here?" I typed his name in the system and waited until his room number popped up.

"I think so. Why? You need me to scare him?"

"202," I said out loud, ignoring Percy's question. I grabbed the spare key and raced around the other side of the counter.

Vance followed close behind me as we made our way up to Theo's room on the second floor.

"Jelly, you didn't answer my question!" Percy floated beside us.

"He gave Aunt Thelma the necklace."

"So, you *do* want me to scare him." Percy's eyes beamed with excitement. "He won't even see me coming!"

"Not yet. Let me talk to him first." I managed to get out while taking the stairs two at a time.

We reached Theo's room, and I knocked on the door, but there was no answer. I tried the doorknob, and it was locked.

"Are you sure he's still here, Percy?" I asked the poltergeist, who floated beside me.

"I don't remember seeing him leave, but there was a spitball incident or two that distracted me." Percy looked thoughtful. "Please hold." Percy didn't wait for a response before he disappeared through the door.

"That's one way to find out if he's here," Vance remarked.

Percy came back moments later. "Oh, Jilly, Jilly, Jilly. This isn't good."

"What? What is it?" Percy couldn't answer me fast enough.

"It's one of those you have to see it to believe it types of things," Percy tried to explain.

I slipped the key in the lock and opened the door.

The room was eerily quiet. The small space was in disarray. Clothes were strewn across the floor, and the bed was unmade. But the most alarming thing was the sight of Theo's lifeless body lying on the ground.

"See what I mean?" Percy hovered over Theo's body. "He's a goner."

"Oh no," I said, my voice barely above a whisper. I trembled as I approached the body. His hand was cold to the touch. It was clear that he had been dead for a while, just as it was clear that he had been murdered. A lamp lay beside him, and from the gash on Theo's head, I'd bet it was the murder weapon.

"We need to call the sheriff," I said, feeling numb.

Vance nodded and pulled out his phone to make the call.

As we waited for the authorities to arrive, I couldn't help but wonder who could have killed Theo and why. Was it someone seeking revenge for the curse on Aunt Thelma, or was there a deeper motive at play? I didn't think it was possible, but this case had taken a turn for the worse.

Deputy Jones was the first to arrive on the scene. He was a seasoned deputy with common sense, and I considered him a friend.

"The Sheriff's out to lunch with Dippy," Deputy Jones said as he walked up to us. "Rumor has it the ice cream man is asking for Amber's hand in marriage."

"Really? He's crazy," I said before I could help myself. It was true, Dippy was a bit of an odd duck, but that's not what I'd meant. I was shocked that he wanted to marry Amber. Deputy Reynolds had grown up a lot over the years, but she was still a drama queen.

"Love must be in the air," Vance smirked. I gave him a playful look that said knock it off. I knew he was talking about Misty and Daniel, but I didn't want anyone else to know.

Deputy Jones didn't ask either one of us for clarification. Instead, he got down to business. "What do we know about the victim?" the deputy motioned to Theo's hotel room.

"His name's Theo. I can't remember his last name off the top of my head. We have it downstairs. He was originally here because of Clemmie," I explained.

"Clemmie?" Deputy Jones asked.

"She met him online. He was her date to Aunt Thelma's birthday party," I added.

"Which is why we wanted to talk to him," Vance motioned to me.

"Libby called from the community center. She has Theo on the security footage, and it looks like he brought the cursed necklace gift. Here, I'll show you." I brought up the video on my phone and turned the screen so the deputy could watch the footage.

"We also talked to Katie at the jewelry store, and she mentioned an older man brought in a necklace earlier in the week. We think it was Theo," Vance said.

"But we haven't confirmed it yet," I admitted.

"Why did Theo want to curse your aunt?" Deputy Jones turned his attention away from the phone.

"That's the million-dollar question, isn't it?" I then thought of something else. "Wait a second. Do you remember what Charity said? She said we needed to catch the culprit to reverse the curse. If he's dead, does that mean the curse can't be reversed?"

"Or maybe it automatically reverses. Remember how all the charms started wearing off at our house?" Vance asked. That I did remember. After we bought our new house, we thought it was falling apart, but it turned out all the home improvement charms were just wearing off after the original owner's death.

"I'm calling the hospital. See if there are any changes in Aunt Thelma." I walked away from Vance and Deputy Jones to place the call.

"Hey, Frederick. How's Aunt Thelma doing? Any changes?" I asked when our lines connected.

Frederick sighed. "No, I'm afraid not. I thought she was going to come to for a minute there, but she must've just been dreaming."

My heart sank at Frederick's words. "I see. Well, listen, we sort of found another piece of the puzzle. Theo, Clemmie's boyfriend, brought the cursed necklace to the party."

"Theo did what now?" Frederick asked.

I repeated the info.

"Well, where is he now?"

"That's the thing. We found him dead in his hotel room."

There was a pause on the other end of the line. "Dead?" Frederick's voice was filled with shock and disbelief.

"Yeah. We're at the scene now with Deputy Jones. We're not sure what happened yet, but we're working on it."

"Who's dead?" Clemmie's voice came through the line from the background. I hadn't realized she was at the hospital. She took the phone from Frederick. "You better start talking," she demanded.

I hesitated, not wanting to upset Clemmie, but I knew she had a right to know. "Theo. I'm sorry," I said gently.

"What! That can't be." Clemmie gasped. "What happened?"

"We're not sure yet," I replied. "We think he was the one who cursed Aunt Thelma, but it looks like he's been..." Again, I wasn't sure how to tell Clemmie the facts without seeming heartless.

"Are you telling me someone offed my boyfriend?" Clemmie seemed to think before adding, "Well, one of them anyway."

"It looks that way." I looked at Vance and grimaced.

There was silence on the other end of the line for a moment before Clemmie spoke again. "I can't believe it. This doesn't make any sense."

"I know. We can't figure it out either."

"Where are you?"

"Mystic Inn."

"Sit tight. I'm headed your way."

I hung up the phone and turned to Vance and Deputy Jones. "Clemmie's on her way. She wants to know what's going on."

They nodded.

"What else do we know about Theo?" Vance asked.

"I don't know. Clemmie knows him the best," I replied.

"You two want to look into him while I get this scene processed?" Deputy Jones asked.

"Yeah, we can do that," I answered for the both of us. Vance and I left the crime scene and headed back downstairs to my office.

"You think there's any chance Theo was just the messenger?" Vance asked.

"What do you mean?"

"That someone gave him the present to deliver," Vance clarified.

I twisted my lips as I thought. "I can buy that. It would explain why he walked right in with the present on full display."

"Right. If you were going to give someone a cursed necklace, wouldn't you have kept it hidden?"

"True, but that doesn't explain him taking the necklace to Katie."

Vance stared out the office window. "I forgot about that."

"Unless it wasn't Theo who took the necklace in?"

"I guess we better find out. What time is it?"

"Six o'clock. The jewelry shop is open for another hour. Want to head back over there?"

"Sure. Then maybe we can grab a bite to eat?"

"And check in on Rocky," I agreed.

As we were about to leave the office, the door burst open, and Clemmie rushed in. I'd honestly forgotten she was on her way over. My mind was clearly all over the place.

"Theo's really dead?" She slapped her hand over her heart.

"He is. I'm so sorry."

"I just can't believe it. He was such a nice man. None of this makes any sense," Clemmie said, shaking her head. "The more I think about it, the more I think he was set up."

"That's what Vance and I were just talking about. Katie recognized the necklace earlier today," I started to say.

"We stopped in the jewelry shop," Vance clarified.

"We were going to see if she recognized Theo. Do you have a picture of him?"

"I sure do." Clemmie pulled out her phone and scrolled through her photos until she found one of her and Theo together. She handed it over to us.

"He didn't seem like the kind of guy who would do something like this," Clemmie said, still in disbelief.

"I'm sure there's more to the story than we know," I agreed as I texted the picture of Theo to my phone. "Do you want to head with us to talk to Katie?"

Clemmie thought for a moment. "You know what. I think I'm just going to sit here for a minute if that's alright with you." Clemmie sat in the leather chair on the other side of my desk.

"Of course. Take all the time you need." I reach over and put a comforting hand on her shoulder before Vance and I left the office to head back to the jewelry store.

On the way over, Vance asked, "Do you really think Theo was set up?"

"I don't know. It's possible, but we need to keep all possibilities in mind until we have all the facts."

"Right. And speaking of facts, what do we know so far?"

"We know that Theo brought the cursed necklace to Aunt Thelma's party, but we don't know why or who gave it to him. We also know that someone, presumably Theo, took the necklace to Katie to add diamonds, but we don't know for sure."

"Why would you swap out sapphires for diamonds if you were going to curse someone?"

"That, I have no idea."

Chapter 12

We arrived at the jewelry store and were relieved to see it was still open. When we walked in, we were greeted by the familiar tinkling sound of the bell over the door. Katie looked up from the counter and smiled.

"Back so soon?" she asked.

"We have a few more questions if you don't mind," I apologized.

"Of course, anything to help."

I pulled out my phone and brought up the picture of Theo. "Is this the man who brought in the necklace?"

Katie took my phone and examined the photo. I held my breath, waiting for her to answer.

"That's him. He was very nice. Trust me, I had no idea what he was up to. I would've never helped if I'd known he was going to curse Thelma."

"Don't worry. We know you wouldn't," I reassured Katie.

"Who is he?" Katie asked.

"His name is Theo Crampton. He was dating Clemmie," Vance answered.

"Jones, that's right. I can't believe I couldn't remember that." I shook my head.

"I haven't seen him since," Katie confirmed.

"And you're not going to. We just found him dead at Mystic Inn." Vance raised his eyebrows.

"Oh my gosh, are you kidding me? This is all nuts. I know you've solved a hundred crimes by now, but I don't know how you do it. I have goosebumps just thinking about it."

I looked over at my husband. "Honestly, we just take it one clue at a time." Vance shrugged in agreement.

"Do you have any idea who did it or why?" Katie's hands were shaking.

"No. But at least we now know that it was his necklace," I said.

Vance looked at me. "And he did intend to give it to Thelma."

I shook my head in disbelief. "Thanks for your help, Katie. I'm sure Deputy Jones or someone from the sheriff's department will want to chat with you."

"Oh. Ok-ay." Katie segmented the word as if she was unsure. "Do you think I need a lawyer or anything? I mean, I did handle the necklace, and now the guy's dead, and your aunt is cursed..." Katie looked between the two of us.

"I can be there with you if you want when they question you," Vance offered.

"Could you? That would be awesome. I'd really appreciate it."

"Sure." Vance took out his business card. "Give me a call when they want to talk to you, and I'll come meet you."

"Thank you. This whole thing makes me super nervous," Katie confessed.

"It's okay. No one thinks you had anything to do with it," I reassured the jeweler.

"Amber's not running the case, is she?" Katie asked.

"No, I don't think so. Why?" I looked at Katie.

"Because she's always quick to accuse people, and now that she's engaged, I'm sure her head will be further in the clouds than it already is. Justice is going to be way low."

"She said yes?" I asked.

"You just missed them. She wanted her ring sized and the center stone enlarged," Katie rolled her eyes.

"Poor Dippy."

"Yep, he's going to be slinging ice cream for the rest of his life," Katie agreed.

After talking with Katie, Vance and I headed next door to the tavern. I felt guilty sitting down for a bite to eat when Aunt Thelma was still unconscious and a killer was out there needing to be caught, but it wouldn't do me any good if I passed out from low blood sugar.

AS WE PERUSED THE MENU, Vance said, "You know, I was thinking about something."

"What's that?" I asked.

"Do we even know if Theo was his real name?" Vance leaned back in his chair.

I raised an eyebrow. "I hadn't thought of that. Why do you ask?"

"Well, think about it. We don't know anything about this guy. Clemmie met him offline. What if he was using a fake name? What if he was working with someone?"

"And that person turned on him and killed him?"

"Or maybe they just used him to do their dirty work and got rid of him when they were done," Vance suggested.

I nodded slowly. "It's a possibility. We need to look into his background and see what we can find."

"Agreed. And we need to keep digging into the curse too. There's got to be more to it than just a necklace."

"Yeah, we need to figure out who's behind it all,"

I said, feeling determined. "But first, let's order some food. I'm starving."

Twenty minutes later, in between bites of my club sandwich and nibbles of french fries I said, "What I can't figure out is, why go after Aunt Thelma? What would Theo have against her? She wasn't keeping Clemmie away from him. As far as I know, he didn't even know her until this past weekend."

Vance nodded thoughtfully. "That's a good point. Maybe it wasn't necessarily about Aunt Thelma. Maybe she was just the easiest target."

I chewed on my sandwich, considering Vance's words. "Maybe. But then why curse her at all? What was the endgame?"

I noticed Clemmie walk in with the older gentleman, and they took a booth in the corner of the tavern. I nudged Vance and nodded in their direction.

"Who's that with Clemmie?" Vance asked.

"I have no idea," I replied.

"Didn't Connie say she'd seen her with a couple of different men?"

"Yeah, she did. I'm trying to figure out how we left her grieving in the office, what, an hour ago, and now she's on a date?"

"I don't know," Vance said, shaking his head. "Maybe she just needed a distraction."

I nodded, understanding. "I get that, but it's just strange timing."

As we finished our meal and got up to leave, I made a detour to Clemmie's table. She seemed uncomfortable when she saw us approaching.

"Hey, Clemmie. Who's your friend?" I asked, nodding to the older gentleman sitting across from her.

Clemmie's smile faltered. "Oh, um, this is ... a friend from out of town," she stammered.

"I see."

Clemmie nodded, still looking uneasy.

"Actually, do you mind if I borrow you for a minute?" I asked, helping Clemmie out of the booth.

Clemmie looked surprised but nodded, getting up from the table. I led her over to a quieter corner of the tavern to talk privately.

"What is going on? You were all upset about Theo a little bit ago, and now you're on a date with another man?"

"It's complicated. Jim's another one of the men I met online who randomly showed up in town. I don't want to seem rude, so I keep being nice to him."

"What about Carl? That was his name, right?" I thought back to the man who'd stopped by the tea shop yesterday morning.

"Thankfully, I haven't run into him. But I did promise him coffee tomorrow morning."

"Clemmie!"

"I know. I know. You warned me this online dating stuff wasn't for the faint of heart. But don't you worry, if they get handsy, I'll turn them into toads, every last one of them." Clemmie patted her purse where I presumed her wand was.

"Are you sure? Do you want us to help get rid of him?" I offered.

"No, I've got it. Don't you worry."

"Well, I am going to worry. Call me when you get home. And lock your doors. And delete your online dating profiles!" I added as she walked away. I could not stand the thought of something bad happening to Clemmie. Images of Aunt Thelma lying in her hospital bed flickered through my mind. They were my undoing.

I followed Clemmie back to her table, where Vance and Jim were talking. "You." I pointed my finger in Jim's face. "Listen up. If you so much as harm a hair on her head, I will curse you back to 1965. I am not kidding. Hasn't anyone ever heard of a phone? Email? Video calling? You don't just show up in someone's town. What is wrong with you?"

"I... I... I thought it was romantic," Jim stammered.

"More like psychotic. I'm keeping my eyes on you."

Sweat beaded on Jim's brow. _Good_, I thought.

"I didn't know. I thought I needed to do something to stand out," Jim confessed to Clemmie.

Chapter 13

After dinner, Vance and I made our way back home to continue our investigation. Rocky greeted us at the door with a bark. He flapped his leathery wings and whipped his devil-like tail as he spun in a circle to say hi. I scratched behind his ear as I walked inside. "Yes, buddy, I'm happy to see you too."

Vance headed straight for the living room with our computers in tow, while I slipped into the kitchen to put on the coffee. Tea wasn't going to cut it. We needed something with more caffeine.

I poured the water into the coffee maker and took a moment to gaze out at the once overgrown rose garden. It had been a mess when we first bought the house, but Vance had worked tirelessly to trim everything back and add to it. Now, the garden was filled with vibrant colors, and the sweet fragrance of the roses wafted in through the open window.

The kitchen had become my favorite room in the house, with its stainless-steel appliances and a wall full of windows that looked out into the backyard. The view was soothing. As the coffee brewed, I walked outside to take a closer look at the garden. Vance had planted new shrubs and flowers, and the trellis that had once been hidden by overgrowth was now covered in climbing roses. The garden had become a sanctuary of sorts, a peaceful escape from the chaos of our investigation.

I thought about the case while I was surrounded by the beauty outside. Again, I wondered if Theo had a partner, and together, they scammed women they met online. There were plenty of online scams where people posed as potential love interests and tricked others into sending them money, like catfishing. The catfisher might use fake photos, fake names, and even fake personal stories to gain the trust of their victim. They may then use this trust to manipulate the victim into giving them money, sensitive personal information, or other resources. The term "catfishing" comes from the idea of using bait to catch fish—in this case, the catfisher is using a fake identity to catch their victim.

It made me wonder if that was what was happening with Clemmie's string of online suitors. Maybe they were all part of a larger scam, and

Clemmie was their latest victim. Did that mean Clemmie's online suitors used her to gain information on Aunt Thelma? Again, I wasn't sure.

There was a real chance I had it all wrong, and Clemmie's boyfriends had nothing to do with Thelma's curse. The real villain could've simply asked Theo to deliver the necklace and then killed him when Theo put two and two together.

But if that was the case, why had Theo taken the necklace to Katie at the jewelry store?

I heard Vance's footsteps behind me and turned to see him walking toward me with a cup of coffee in hand. He smiled as he handed it to me. "You figure it all out yet?"

"Not even in close, but the garden is beautiful," I replied, taking a sip of the hot coffee.

Vance shrugged modestly. "It's a gift," he joked.

"One I'm thankful for."

Vance smiled, then took my hand and led me back inside. We settled in on the couches with our coffees and computers while I filled Vance in on my thoughts.

"I don't know, maybe my skepticism towards online dating has clouded my judgment." But even as I said those words, I couldn't help but think of all the true crime stories I'd watched where the victim had met their attacker online. My comment led us off on a tangent, talking about the recent online scams and crimes we'd each heard about. We both felt it was a fine line between trying to embrace technology yet protect ourselves at the same time.

"But back to Theo, I don't think your judgment is clouded at all. It would be one thing if he had only delivered the necklace. But the fact that he paid to have diamonds put into it shows he's more than the messenger."

"Isn't that weird, though? Why would you put diamonds into something you were going to curse?"

"Yeah, that doesn't make any sense. You think you'd curse a piece of costume jewelry."

"Right, and he didn't try to hide it—any of it. He had a jeweler in Silverlake customize the piece, and he walked right into the community center with the necklace on full display." I sighed in frustration.

"We need to look into Theo more."

"We do," I agreed.

"Let's start there and see where it takes us."

I took a deep pull of coffee, thankful it had since cooled, before setting my mug down, "Let's do this."

In a short amount of time, Vance had managed to run a background check and pull up plenty of intel on Theo. "He retired from the army," he said. "He was a colonel. He served in the Gulf War."

I typed away on my laptop, trying to find more information as well. "And he's from Fernandina Beach in northern Florida."

"He's divorced," Vance continued reading. "Ex-wife has since passed." Vance continued to scroll down on the screen. "He has one adult daughter, Maya Crampton."

"Maya Crampton, huh?" I said, taking note of the name. "I wonder if she knows about her dad's death?"

"I'm not sure," Vance said, "but it's worth a shot to find out." He started searching for a phone number for Maya while I continued to look up information on Theo. I struck paydirt when I found a recent interview in the American Legion Magazine. "Vance, listen to this," I said, reading from my laptop.

Theo Crampton, a retired colonel of the US Army, was a highly decorated officer who received numerous honors for his service, including the Humanitarian Service Medal. However, after retiring from the military, he struggled to adjust to civilian life and suffered from PTSD. In a talk he gave at a local American Legion, Theo spoke candidly about his struggles and his journey toward recovery.

"I had a tough time adjusting to civilian life," Theo said. "I missed the structure and camaraderie of the military. I turned to alcohol to cope, and it almost destroyed me."

Despite his struggles, Theo sought help and attended a rehabilitation program, where he became sober. He then began volunteering at a local veterans' organization in Fernandina Beach, where he found a renewed sense of purpose.

"Volunteering has given me a way to give back to my fellow veterans," Theo said. "It's helped me stay sober and find meaning in my life."

Theo's story is a reminder that the transition from military to civilian life can be challenging for many veterans. It also highlights the importance of seeking help and support when facing mental health struggles.

As Theo said, "There's no shame in asking for help. We all need it at some point in our lives."

"What do you think? It sounds like he was a decent guy who fell on hard times but turned his life around."

"Yeah, what medal did it say he earned?"

I rescanned the article. "The Humanitarian Service Medal."

Vance typed the award into his computer, "It's an individual service medal awarded by the US Department of Defense for aiding in humanitarian acts such as natural disaster relief, evacuation of noncombatants from a hostile area, or humanitarian support to refugees."

"Okay, if that's true, then cursing my aunt seems out of character."

"It does, which is why I'm glad I found Maya's number. I'm going to call her and see what she says."

Vance dialed the number and put his phone on speaker. After the phone rang several times, a generic voicemail greeting picked up. I didn't blame Maya for letting the call go to voicemail. I never answered unknown numbers, either. Hopefully, she'd call us back once she listened to the message.

Vance was still engrossed in his research, so I decided to call Frederick and see how Aunt Thelma was doing and if he had that list of names we talked about earlier. I grabbed my phone and dialed his number, waiting for him to pick up.

"Hello?" Frederick's voice was gruff and tired.

"Hey, Frederick, it's Angelica. How are you holding up?" I asked.

"I'm hanging in there. Just praying Thelma wakes up soon."

"How is she doing?"

"She's the same," Frederick said with a heavy sigh. "But I'm not leaving her side until she's awake."

"Thank you for that. Sorry, I haven't been up there."

"No, you don't need to apologize. What you're doing is far more important."

"You need to make sure you're taking care of yourself, too."

"Don't worry, I am. I left for a little bit to get cleaned up and grab a bite to eat. Robert stayed with her while I was out."

"Oh, well, that's … good," I was surprised to hear the two men were getting along so well, but I wasn't about to say so. "Listen, did you ever write up a list of political enemies or people who might have a grudge against you?" I asked.

"I sure do. I left them with Percy at the inn when I passed through," he said.

"Oh, okay. It must've been after I left. I'll swing by there tomorrow and pick it up." I felt a twinge of guilt for leaving Percy and Eleanor to run things. I owed the two of them some time off, big time. But first, we needed to find out if there was any connection between Theo and any potential suspects, anyone who could've taken advantage of him.

After thanking Frederick for staying with Aunt Thelma, I hung up with him and relayed the conversation to Vance, who nodded in agreement. "Sounds good. I'll keep digging," he said, his fingers flying over his keyboard.

I took a sip of my coffee and settled into the couch, scrolling through my own computer. Rocky hopped next to my lap and settled in for a nap. At least one of us was going to get some sleep tonight.

Chapter 14

The next morning, as I left my house and made my way to Mystic Inn, I noticed that the sky was ominously cloudy. The air felt thick and heavy, and the wind had a certain edge to it. I couldn't help but feel like a storm was brewing, like nature itself was gearing up to unleash some kind of fury upon us.

As I arrived at the inn, I was greeted by the sound of the wind howling through the trees and the sight of the leaves whipping around wildly. Waves rippled across the lake. No one was out fishing this morning.

Once inside, I made my way to the front desk to check in with Percy. He was busy answering the phone, so I waited patiently for him to finish. As he hung up, he looked up at me and smiled.

"Morning, Jilly," he said. "It's a spooky one out

there today, huh?" He looked thrilled with the ominous weather. "How's Thelma?"

"The same."

"Well, that's rotten." His jolly attitude shifted.

I nodded in agreement. "That it is. Listen, do you have a list of names from Frederick?"

Percy rummaged through the papers on his desk before producing a sheet of paper. "Right here. Frederick gave this to me yesterday. Said it might be helpful."

I took the paper from Percy's outstretched hand and quickly scanned the names. None of them stood out to me, but that wasn't surprising. "Thanks, Percy. Have you seen Carl around this morning? He's still a guest, right?"

"Carl, Carl, Carl … not ringing a bell."

"He's a friend of Clemmie's. Carl Kieff. Older man, tall, nice gray hair that he keeps styled to the side." I tried to think of how else to describe Boyfriend Number Two, as I was starting to mentally refer to them. Theo had been Number One, and Jim was Number Three.

"Uh-huh, and how many friends does Clemmie have?" Percy used air quotes around the word *friends*.

I tried not to sigh when replying, "A few. Carl stopped by the tea shop with flowers two days ago, and I want to chat with him." Maybe he had a military connection with Theo?

"Oh, that guy. Now I know who you mean. He's in room 12. I haven't seen him this morning, though. Want me to give him a call and see if he's around?"

"That would be great, thanks."

Percy picked up the phone and dialed Carl's room number. I stood there, tapping my foot impatiently as I waited for Percy to finish the call. Finally, he hung up and turned to me. "No answer, but I can zip on over and take a peekie poo."

"Wait! Hold up." I twisted my lips in thought. Normally, I respected guests' privacy. I wasn't one to send a ghost into someone's room every time they didn't answer the phone. Yesterday with Theo had been an exception. I didn't want to give Percy the idea that I expected him to drop in on guests all the time. That would be a disaster.

"Let's grab the spare key and pay him a visit the old-fashioned way." Percy cocked his head, not following me. "By knocking," I supplied.

"Oh, knocking. Right, right. I knew that." Percy lowered his voice. "Completely boring and useless when you can walk through walls," he said to himself.

Percy followed me as we made the short trip down the hall.

"Carl?" I called out, rapping my knuckles on the wooden door. "It's Angelica, the manager of Mystic Inn. Can I talk to you?"

We waited a couple of minutes.

"Now, can I go in?" Percy raised his eyebrows.

"Hang on."

Percy sighed so loudly that I turned and gave him my full attention. "All I'm saying is the guy could be dead as a doornail, and you have us standing out here like a couple of mortals." Percy raised his eyebrows.

The image of Theo lying dead on the floor came flooding back to me.

I wasted no time inserting the key into the lock and turning it. The door clicked open, and I cautiously stepped inside. "Carl, are you here?"

Silence greeted me.

The room was tidy, with a queen-sized bed in the center of the room and a dresser, and small TV against the wall. The curtains were drawn, casting the room in dim light, and the air conditioner hummed along the back wall.

"Well, that's disappointing," Percy folded his hands across his chest.

"That he's not dead?"

"You have to admit, yesterday was exciting."

I closed my eyes and shook my head. When I opened them, Percy had vanished.

"Do you need something?" Eleanor asked from the open door behind me. "I just passed Percy. He was griping about something."

"No dead body," I replied.

"Percy!" His wife hollered after him. I could tell Eleanor wanted to make an excuse for her husband. She started and stopped her sentence a time or two.

"Don't worry about it. We all know how he is."

"He's very sweet."

"We know."

Eleanor floated after her husband, and I took a final walk around the room.

Carl's suitcase was still on the luggage rack. His toiletries were still in the bathroom, and the towels were damp, indicating that Carl had recently taken a shower. It looked like he had been in the room of late, but he was nowhere to be found. The bed was made, and there were no signs of a struggle or anything out of the ordinary. I wondered where he could have gone on such a dreary day like today.

"Wait, wasn't he going to meet Clemmie?" I spoke to myself. I took out my phone and sent Clemmie a quick text, seeing if she was with Carl and if we could meet up, then I walked back out to the lobby.

As I made my way to the front desk, I heard Percy talking to a young woman.

"Hi, excuse me," she said, her voice shaking as she wiped away her tears. "I'm looking for information about my father, Theo Crampton. I was told he had stayed here." The woman looked to be in her midthirties, with long brown hair and tear-stained cheeks. I recognized her from the photo Vance had found on Theo's social media profile.

Percy looked at her kindly and smiled. "Oh yes, the corpse on the second floor. How may I help you?"

Maya choked out a sob, cutting off her words.

"Percy!" I rushed forward to help.

Percy puckered his lips in confusion. "Was it something I said?" he whispered to me while I comforted Maya. My look should have said it all. Percy shrugged his shoulders and floated away.

"Sorry, Percy's not the most eloquent of employees." I handed a tissue over to Theo's daughter. "My name's Angelica, and this is my family's inn. I tried to call you last night."

Maya looked up at me, her eyes red and swollen. "I'm sorry. It's been … a lot." Maya visibly swallowed.

"I understand."

Maya pressed on. "The police called me last night too, but they wouldn't tell me anything. I don't understand what happened."

"That's what we're trying to find out. Do you have a couple of moments to talk? If you would like some time to get settled, I can understand that." Maya was so emotionally distraught; I didn't want to add to her distress.

"No, that's okay. I want to talk." Maya looked around the lobby. While it was decorated comfortably, with two sofas and plenty of throw pillows, it wasn't the place to have such a private, emotionally charged conversation.

"Here, why don't you come upstairs with me. My aunt has an apartment where we can talk."

"I can do that." Maya agreed and followed me upstairs to the third floor.

"You want any tea or anything?" I said once we were inside.

"Um, I guess tea would be great." Maya looked around my apartment, which looked like a time capsule from the 1960s with pink shag carpet and plenty of gold accents.

"Do you know what your dad was doing in Silverlake?" I asked while putting the electric kettle on.

"When I talked to him last week, he told me he was visiting a friend. But I never did get the name. Dad was always going off on a trip here or there. He liked to visit friends, old army buddies. Stuff like that. It was hard to keep track of everything."

I nodded to show that I was listening while still moving around Aunt Thelma's kitchen. I took down the sugar bowl and got out the cream and a few cookies to complete the spread.

"I see. Well, he was in town visiting friends. Her name is Clemmie, and she is a very nice lady."

Maya's demeanor completely changed.

"A woman did this? Don't tell me he met her

online. I was always telling him he couldn't trust people on the internet. Do you know how much money he's lost to computer scams? He gets taken advantage of left and right no matter how many times I talked to him."

I tried to backtrack. "Clemmie's not to blame. She's a dear friend of mine. I've known her for decades."

Maya looked skeptical but, after a few moments, said, "I guess I don't understand."

I wanted to tell her that was okay because I didn't really understand it all either, but instead, I switched tactics. I took out my phone and brought up a picture of the necklace and turned to show it to her. "Does this look familiar to you?"

Maya's expression paled. "Where did you get this?" she took the phone from my hand and zoomed in to get a closer look.

"Your dad gave it to my aunt."

"Clemmie, is your aunt?"

"No, Clemmie is my aunt's best friend. Your dad was Clemmie's date to my aunt's birthday party on Saturday. What can you tell me about the necklace?"

Maya took a shaky breath. "It was my grandmother's. It looked a bit different back then. I don't know what the exact gemstones were, but they weren't diamonds."

The water began to boil I walked over to pour it

into the teapot. "That's right. Your dad had it customized at the jewelry store in town."

"And he gave it to your aunt?" I could tell that Maya was skeptical.

"That's right, but it gets even stranger." When my aunt opened the gift Sunday morning, she was cursed. She's been in the hospital ever since."

Maya gasped. "What? I don't understand. My father wouldn't curse anyone. And why would he give your aunt such an expensive piece of jewelry?"

"That's what we're trying to figure out."

"My dad wouldn't have cursed your aunt. I can promise you that. He hated violence. That's why the war was so hard on him. He tried to save so many lives over there. For a long time, it broke him. He had just finally gotten his life back together. He was volunteering, taking care of himself, looking for love." A fresh batch of tears spilled down Maya's cheeks.

As I sat and talked with Maya, she continued to defend her father's innocence. She claimed that someone must have set him up or that he was under the influence of some sort of spell. I admitted the idea hadn't occurred to me before. But then again, Vance and I both knew that anything was possible in a town like Silverlake.

"I understand how you feel," I said sympathetically. "But is it possible that he was in the wrong place at the wrong time or that he got mixed up with the wrong people?"

Maya shook her head vehemently. "No, it's not possible. My dad wouldn't do anything like that. He was retired, he was living a quiet life. He was trying to put his past behind him." I nodded, knowing I wasn't going to get anywhere with this line of questioning. "My dad didn't deserve to die like this. He was a good man," she continued.

After a few more moments of conversation, I offered Maya a room at Mystic Inn. "I know it's not much, but you're more than welcome to stay here with us for a while. We have plenty of space, and I'd be happy to help you in any way I can."

But Maya shook her head, "I can't stay here. Not where my dad ... you know." Her voice trailed off, and I could see tears welling up in her eyes once again.

I understood her hesitancy and quickly suggested an alternative. "How about the bed-and-breakfast in town? It's run by a lovely lady, and it's a peaceful place to stay. I can give you her contact information, and she'll take good care of you."

Maya nodded, "Thank you, I appreciate that." She wiped away a tear with the back of her hand, and I could see the weight of the world on her shoulders. "You're not alone in this," I said, offering her a reassuring smile. "We'll get to the bottom of it, I promise."

Chapter 15

After saying goodbye to Maya, I couldn't help but feel a sense of sadness. Her defense of her father's innocence had given me a lot to think about. I walked through Aunt Thelma's apartment, knowing I was missing something. I scanned the room, looking for anything out of place or anything that might give me a clue about what had happened. Why had she been targeted?

But everything looked the same as it had before. The furniture, a mix of vintage pieces that had been around since the decade itself, was in its usual place. Over on the windowsill, I saw that the plants were starting to wilt. A combination of summer sun and a lack of water would do that. The plants were in a variety of pots, ranging from small and simple to large and ornate, each one unique. The window itself was large, letting in plenty of natural light. I'd read a recent article in the Smithsonian Magazine that pants cried when they were hurt or thirsty. Sure, it's a supersonic cry that humans couldn't hear, but the fact was unnerving enough for me to water them pronto. I fetched the pitcher from the kitchen to give them a drink, talking to them in the process. "Don't worry, Aunt Thelma will be home soon," I reassured them, hoping my voice and water were enough to perk them back up.

As I moved around the apartment, I couldn't help but admire the original 1960s decor. The pink shag carpet was bold and unique, matching the gold accents that adorned the furniture and accessories. A coffee table made of heavy, dark wood sat in front of the couch, adorned with a vase of fresh flowers that had long since wilted. I decided to toss the flowers as well, which was a smart move as no one thought to take out the trash from Sunday.

As I made my way to the kitchen to take out the trash, I noticed the utility and cable bills sitting on the counter. Aunt Thelma had always been meticulous about paying her bills on time, and I didn't want that to change. I opened the bills and made a note of the due dates. I was already joint on her bank accounts, so I could write the checks for her and drop them in the mail, which meant I needed to find her checkbook. The thing about Aunt Thelma is she's notorious for misplacing things. Her checkbook was no exception. Luckily, I'd gotten pretty good at casting summoning charms, such as Éla edó. In order for this spell to work, you have to have the object clearly in your mind when summoning it.

I took out my wand, closed my eyes, and took a deep breath, focusing my mind on Aunt Thelma's checkbook. It was made of bright, floral-patterned fabric and had a pen holder attached to it, along with a small pocket for receipts. As I recited the incantation, "Éla edó," I could feel the magic coursing through me, and I pictured the checkbook in my mind's eye.

Suddenly, I heard a whooshing sound, and I opened my eyes to see the checkbook flying through the air, heading straight for me. I caught it deftly with one hand, a satisfied smile spreading across my face.

My joy faded once I flipped through the checkbook. The register didn't make sense. I couldn't figure out where some of the entries came from, and the handwriting was hard to decipher. It looked like there were some withdrawals that I couldn't account for and a few large deposits that didn't make sense.

That's when I saw her bank statement tucked in with the mail. I opened it up and scanned through the pages, my eyes widening as I saw the numbers. The balance was much higher than I had anticipated, and there were several large deposits made in the past few months. I knew that she had inherited money when a friend died two years ago, but this was more than I expected. I couldn't help but wonder where all this money came from. Could she have been a financial mark? And where did she get all this money from?

As I was putting away Aunt Thelma's checkbook, I heard a faint noise and turned around to see Eleanor floating through the door.

"Do you need any help, dearie?" she asked, her spectral form flickering in and out of view.

I looked around the apartment at the wilted flowers and the trash bag I had just filled. "I was just cleaning up the place."

Eleanor floated over to the window and looked at the plants. "Don't worry about it. Leave it to me to clean up," she said kindly. "I'll take care of everything."

"You don't have to."

"Hush now, it's my job."

"Cleaning the inn is, but not this."

"It's no trouble," the sweet ghost assured me.

"Thank you, Eleanor," I said gratefully. "I really appreciate it."

Eleanor smiled, her eyes crinkling with warmth. I debated for a second bringing up Aunt Thelma's bank account, but Eleanor wouldn't know anything about it. The person I needed to talk with was Clemmie, and she still hadn't texted me back or called me. I tried to call her right then and there, and she didn't answer her phone. I didn't like that one bit.

I quickly dialed Diane's number next, hoping she would answer. After a few rings, she picked up.

"Is everything okay?" I could hear the soft clatter of dishes, the hiss of the cappuccino machine, and the gentle hum of conversation that made up the cozy atmosphere of Diane's bakery.

"Do you know where Clemmie is?" I asked.

"No, haven't seen her. Why?"

"She was supposed to meet Carl for coffee, but I haven't talked to her since."

"The guy she hid from at the tea shop?"

"That's the one. Ever since Theo turned up dead yesterday, my mind's been working overtime. I'm worried one of her online boyfriends had some-thing to do with it. Maybe they were working together? I don't know. Theo's daughter, Maya, thinks her dad was set up or even spelled."

"Wait, wait, wait! Hang on a minute. Theo is dead?"

"You didn't know that? Where have you been?"

"I worked all day yesterday. Mayor Parrish requested a rush-order, three-layer birthday cake for her nephew, and Frederick didn't say anything when I was visiting Thelma this morning."

I took a minute to recap the past twenty-four hours, including finding the extra money in Aunt Thelma's account.

"Well, you're right. I don't know anything about that. But your aunt did talk to Roger a time or two about investing. I tuned the conversation out as I have no clue when it comes to that sort of thing."

"Okay, when you talk to him, will you ask him to give me a call?"

"Sure thing. I'll keep my eye out for Clemmie, too."

"Okay, thank you."

After hanging up with Diane, I decided to head to Clemmie's tea shop to see if she was there. I called ahead, but there was no answer. Outside, the morning storm had blown through, leaving branches and debris scattered across the road. I made the quick drive to Village Square, thankful it wasn't the weekend and that I could easily find a parking spot.

Walking into the tea shop, the sweet aroma of tea filled the air. Clemmie was dancing with a broom in her hand, sweeping the floor with a contented expression on her face. As I got closer, I saw she was listening to music. The white piece of her earphones was just barely visible underneath her dark hair.

I walked up to Clemmie, who hadn't noticed me yet and tapped her on the shoulder. She jumped and turned around, a surprised look on her face.

"Oh, silver stars! You startled me! Don't you

know not to sneak up on old people? You'll kill us flat out with a heart attack."

"Where have you been? I've called and texted. You're not answering anything."

"What's happened?" Clemmie took out her earbuds. "Did you catch the bad guy? Is Thelma awake?"

"No, and no. And I'm worried you might be in danger. Weren't you meeting up with Carl today?"

"He was a no-show, and I am completely fine with that. Jim seems like a nice man; I'm going to date him for a bit. I took your advice, too, and deleted my profile. I do not have the mental energy for dating multiple men."

"What do you mean he was a no-show?"

"Like I said, he stood me up, and Clemmie doesn't track no man down."

"Okay, that's fine, but listen, I'm trying to find him to interview him. Did you ever tell these guys about Aunt Thelma or talk about money?"

"Of course, I talked about Thelma. She's my best friend, isn't she? But no, we never talked about finances. That's nobody's business except my own. Well, and Thelma's. We talked money all the time."

I looked around the shop to see if any of her customers were listening. Most of them were over on the other side of the shop enjoying their brew with a sweet treat seeing the tea shop was divided into two sections. On one side, there were shelves lined with various homey gifts and tea accessories, and on the other, there were tables where customers could sit for a spell.

I kept my voice low. "You two talked money?"

"Of course. I bought Bitcoin at fifty cents!" Clemmie looked pleased as punch, but I had no idea what she was talking about.

"It's not my moon bag, but it's something."

"Moon bag?"

"You know, the crypto coins I'm holding that will make me rich. To the moon!"

I blinked. "You guys invest in crypto?"

"You don't?"

"Um, no." Crypto was violate. I preferred slow, safe growth—like bonds. "So that's where Aunt Thelma got her money?"

"She was smart and cashed out at the coin's all-time high. Meanwhile, I'm over here holding the bag, but it'll go up again, mark my words." I understood half of what Clemmie said.

"Okay, so if I've got this right, Aunt Thelma made her money from investing in crypto, but does anyone else know that?"

"What are you thinking?"

"Well, Maya, that's Theo's daughter." I honestly couldn't remember who knew what at this point. "Thinks her dad was set up or even spelled into cursing Aunt Thelma. I'm wondering if Theo was working with someone—"

"Like a partner?"

"Exactly, and that partner turned on him and killed him after Aunt Thelma was cursed. I'm going to head to the bank now and make sure all of the funds are in her account."

"Are you thinking Carl killed Theo and ran off with Thelma's money?"

"I'm thinking it's a possibility." The theory didn't fully explain everything, but it was the best that I had.

"Alright, I'm stuck here unless I can get one of my girls to come in early. Let me make some calls, and I'll see what I can do."

"Okay, keep me posted."

"I'll keep trying to track down Carl, too."

"Okay, I'll talk to you shortly."

<hr>

Chapter 16

<hr>

I made my way to the bank, eager to check on Aunt Thelma's account. As I walked through the doors, I spotted Molly McCormick, a friend from high school who worked there. She was chatting with a customer, but as soon as she saw me, she rushed over with a big smile on her face.

"Well, well, well! Look who it is! Haven't seen you in ages, Angelica," Molly said, giving me a big hug.

"Hi, Molly. How are you?" I replied, trying to steer the conversation toward business.

"Oh, you know, same old same old. Work, home, sleep, repeat. But enough about me. I heard about your poor aunt. Such a tragedy," she said, her expression turning solemn.

"Yes, it is," I agreed. "Actually, that's why I'm here—"

Molly's eyes lit up, and she launched into a story involving Silverlake's favorite mischievous teenage twins, Beatrice and Sabrina.

"Speaking of tragedies," she continued, "have you heard about the magical prank Beatrice and Sabrina pulled last week?"

"Oh no, what happened?" I asked, intrigued. I was half afraid to ask. Beatrice and Sabrina were a dynamic duo whose idea of fun often backfired.

"Well, I don't know if you know, but they've been studying potions lately. Connie's been tutoring them."

"She has?" *What is she thinking?* I thought to myself.

"Apparently, they brewed up a truth serum and slipped it into the lemonade at the church potluck. They thought it would be hilarious. But things didn't go exactly as planned."

"Oh no," I said, already knowing where this was going.

"Yeah, turns out the serum was a bit stronger than they thought. Half the town was suddenly confessing to all sorts of wild things. Reverend Johnson admitted to stealing candy from the corner store when he was ten, and Mrs. Jenkins confessed to putting a curse on her ex-husband's new girl-friend. It was chaos!"

I couldn't help but chuckle at the image of half

the town suddenly revealing their deepest, darkest secrets. Molly always knew how to liven up a conversation. She was the town's unofficial news source.

Finally, after what seemed like an eternity, Molly paused to take a breath. I seized the opportunity to redirect the conversation.

"So, about Aunt Thelma's account..." I trailed off, hoping to finally get some answers.

"Oh, right, yes. Follow me. Did you hear I'm the new branch manager?" Molly led me into an office off to the side of the teller lobby. I'd been in this office a time or two with the previous manager, and let's just say our meeting hadn't ended well. I tried to let the past go as I sat across from Molly.

"So, what would you like to know?"

"For starters, I saw a recent bank statement, and I just wanted to make sure my aunt's account was secure."

Molly finally got back to business and pulled up Aunt Thelma's account on her computer. "Looks like the balance is the same as usual," she said, pointing at the screen. "I talked to your aunt about opening multiple accounts to ensure her excess deposits but looks like she hasn't moved anything over."

"Excess deposits?"

"Right. Your account is insured up to two

hundred and fifty thousand. Anything after that, you're not insured unless you spread your money out over multiple institutions, or you add more additional joint account owners."

"So, because I'm on the account, the protection goes up?" I clarified.

"Right, each account owner is covered for the two-hundred fifty thousand. If there are two account owners, it's half a million dollars. Let me check something." Molly clicked away on the keyboard. "Oh, I stand corrected. Your aunt added another account owner."

"She did? Who?"

"Frederick Kringle? Isn't that the man she's seeing?"

"Yes." I nodded, unable to say another word. That was odd, Aunt Thelma never combined finances. Not even with her previous husbands.

"So that increased her account protection." Molly smiled as if that was the greatest news ever, but something didn't sit right with me. I started to wonder if maybe Uncle Robert was right, and we shouldn't trust Frederick.

Then again, he had never done anything to make me question his motives. "Thanks, Molly. I appreciate your help," I said as I got up to leave. As I did, my phone rang in my purse. It was Clemmie. "If you'll excuse me, I have to take this call."

Molly waved goodbye, and I stepped outside the office.

"Hello?"

I barely got the word out of my mouth before Clemmie shouted, "I've been robbed!"

I quickly pulled the phone away from my ear, wincing at Clemmie's volume. "What? Slow down, Clemmie. What do you mean you've been robbed?"

"All the money is missing from my account!" Clemmie replied, still talking so fast that it was hard for me to keep up. "I decided to check online after our talk, and when I logged in, I saw that my money was missing! All of it!"

"Oh no. Where are you at right now?"

"Freaking out at the tea shop is where I'm at. I'm waiting for Ginny to get here so I can hightail it to the bank!"

"I'm at the bank right now. Do you want me to wait for you?"

"Can you do that?"

"Of course."

"Good. Tell them I'm on my way. I'll be there as fast as I can."

I poked my head back into Molly's office and relayed the message.

Molly immediately got to work, typing on her keyboard. "Let me check the account activity," she said, her fingers flying over the keys.

When Clemmie arrived, Molly was ready to get right to work.

"When was the last time you checked your balance, Clemmie?"

"I don't know, a few days ago?" Clemmie replied.

"Okay, here it is. There's been a large transfer out of the account just this morning," Molly said, pointing at the screen. "It was transferred to a different bank."

"A different bank?" I repeated, feeling a knot form in my stomach. This was getting worse by the minute.

"Yes, it looks like it was transferred to First National Bank of Riverdale," Molly said, squinting at the screen.

"I don't even have an account there!" Clemmie exclaimed.

"I'll file a fraud claim," Molly said, her voice calm and professional. "We'll get this sorted out for you. Do you have any idea how this could have happened?"

"No, I don't," Clemmie said, sounding panicked. "I mean, I know I've used my card to buy things online, but I've never had any issues before."

"Okay, let's get this claim filed and go from there," Molly said, clicking away on the keyboard again. "I'll also put a hold on your account to prevent any further transactions."

"I appreciate that. Good thing they didn't get my moon bag," Clemmie said to me.

"Now let's call over to First National Bank and ask them to put a hold on things from their end," Molly said, picking up the phone.

Molly dialed the number for First National Bank of Riverdale and was transferred several times before she finally reached the manager. She listened intently, her expression growing more and more serious with each passing moment.

"Okay, thank you," Molly said finally. She hung up the phone and turned to Clemmie and me. "I'm sorry to say this, but the money has already been withdrawn."

Clemmie gasped. "What? How is that possible?"

Molly shook her head. "Unfortunately, it's a known scam. You don't even need magic. If a con artist is able to reset your bank password, they can change your login credentials and move money around in minutes. It happens so fast that we can rarely catch them."

"That's terrible," I said, feeling a sense of anger rising within me. "Doesn't the FDIC protect you?" I asked, hoping for some good news.

Molly shook her head. "Unfortunately, the FDIC doesn't cover fraud. But don't worry, our bank has separate insurance for cases like this. Let me go get the paperwork, and we'll get started."

"If Carl did this, so help me, I'm turning him

into the steaming pile of dog poo he is," Clemmie said, her fists clenching.

"Let's not jump to any conclusions just yet," I cautioned her, even though I felt she was probably right.

"Okay then," Molly returned with a stack of paperwork. "Let's start by filling out this fraud claim. We'll also need to contact the police and file a report."

Clemmie nodded, her expression grim. "Let's do it."

As Clemmie started filling out the paperwork, my phone rang. It was Mystic Inn.

Again, I excused myself and stepped outside of the office.

"Hello?"

"It's Eleanor," came the ghostly voice on the other end of the line.

"Eleanor? Is everything okay?" I asked, surprised to be hearing from her. Eleanor never called me.

"Yes, everything is fine. But I found something interesting while I was cleaning up your aunt's apartment."

"What is it?"

"Under the couch, I found a gift tag."

"A gift tag? What does it say?"

"It says 'To Clemmie, from Theo.'" Eleanor replied as if she was reading it again. "There's a bit of blue wrapping paper stuck to the back of it. Not sure if that matters."

Oh, it mattered. My throat suddenly felt very dry as Eleanor spoke. The cursed necklace had been wrapped in blue wrapping paper.

"Percy mentioned something about a necklace coming from Theo, right?" Eleanor continued.

"Yes, he did, but we thought he'd given it to Aunt Thelma." The idea of the necklace being a gift from Theo to Clemmie made perfect sense, and I wondered why we didn't consider it before.

Clemmie quit filling out the forms and looked over at me. I didn't know how to tell her that she'd been the intended victim, not Thelma.

I bought myself time by thanking Eleanor for the information and telling her I'd swing by the inn shortly to grab it. It was only after hanging up that I walked back into the office to fill Clemmie in. Only this wasn't a conversation I wanted to have in front of Molly. I wasn't ready for all of Silverlake to hear the latest break in the case.

"Can you give us a minute?" I asked Molly.

Molly hesitated for a moment, her eyes flickering with unspoken questions. If she wasn't curious before, she was now. But Molly was too much of a professional to refuse.

"Of course," Molly gave a small nod and stood up from her desk. She grabbed a file folder and walked out of the office, giving us a polite smile on her way out.

I waited until she was out the door before saying, "Do you remember how the necklace didn't have a gift tag?"

"This is about the necklace?" Clemmie looked incredulous.

"Yes, what did you think it was about?"

"I thought Thelma had died the way the color drained from your face. Good heavens child, you almost gave me a heart attack."

"I still might when you hear what I have to say. So, you remember the necklace missing the name tag?"

"Right, I remember that."

"Well, it turns out it did have a tag. It had just fallen under the couch. The necklace was from Theo, but it was addressed to you."

"Say what now?" It was a rhetorical question. Clemmie heard me loud and clear. "You telling me that not only did Carl drain my bank account, but Theo tried to curse me too?"

"More like they worked together, and Carl killed Theo and took off with the money." That was my theory, anyway.

"That ain't happening. One way or another, we are going to find that man." Clemmie stood up, leaving the half-filled-out papers behind. "We'll be back for these," Clemmie said toward the open door where she knew Molly could hear her.

The bank manager poked her head back in.

"No problem, ladies. I'll have them waiting for you." I knew Molly was dying to ask questions, but we didn't give her a chance as we hightailed it out of the bank.

Chapter 17

Clemmie pulled her wand out and rested it on her lap while I pulled out of the parking lot. She scanned the streets for any sign of Carl. We were in the business district where most residents worked. On this side of the lake were the schools, post office, courthouse, sheriff's department, doctors' offices—things like that. The other side of the lake was more for tourism with the Village Square shops, Bed & Breakfast, and Mystic Inn.

"Stop the car!" Clemmie exclaimed as I pulled up to the only light in town.

I slammed on the brakes, and Clemmie jumped out of the car. A streak of orange light shone brightly as it shot out of Clemmie's wand, engulfing the man's shoes and hardening them in an instant. The man stumbled forward, the weight of his cement shoes keeping him on his feet.

I gaped at Clemmie, unable to believe what had just happened. Even I could tell from inside the car that the man wasn't Carl.

Mr. McCormick, Molly's dad and one of the town council members, was in a desperate struggle to stay upright. His feet were rooted to the ground, and his arms were outstretched, flailing as he tried to maintain his balance. I ran out of the car to help him.

"Sorry, Mike!" Clemmie shouted, followed by the countercurse, *tixie*. The cement shoes instantly vanished, and Mike staggered forward. I caught him just in time.

Clemmie turned to me, her cheeks flushed with embarrassment. "I thought it was Carl."

"I figured as much."

"I'm sorry," Clemmie repeated to Mr. McCormick. "I thought you were someone else."

Thankfully, Mr. McCormick had a good sense of humor. "Who were you trying to curse?" he asked instead of laying into Clemmie.

"A friend of mine from online." Clemmie looked at me like she dared me to contradict her. I wanted to remind Clemmie that if she didn't want people involved in her personal business, she couldn't go around cursing them downtown, but I kept my mouth shut.

"Must be some friend," Mr. McCormick chuckled. "I'm headed to the post office, and then I think

I'll head home until you catch your bad guy. Give me a call when you do."

"Sure thing, Mike."

"Bye, Mr. McCormick," I added, and I tugged Clemmie's arm to hurry back in the car. I was only halfway pulled over. The back end of my vehicle was sticking out a bit. Cars had to keep going around.

"That was embarrassing," Clemmie said while clipping her seat belt. "But you have to admit Mike looks an awful lot like Carl."

"No, he doesn't. They both have gray hair, and that's about it."

"And they're both men."

"That's a given, but if you cursed every man with gray hair, you'd have to curse half of Silver-lake's population."

"It'd be a start," Clemmie quipped.

"Oh, Clemmie," I groaned. "Put your wand away until we get to the inn."

"You put your wand away. I'm keeping mine out." Clemmie looked back out the window. "He's here somewhere," she whispered.

I shook my head and kept on driving.

The second we got to the inn, I called Deputy Jones to tell him about the gift tag.

"Turns out we had it wrong. Clemmie was the target, not Aunt Thelma."

"How so?" Deputy Jones asked.

"We found the gift tag. A bit of the wrapping paper is still stuck to the tape. Clemmie's bank account has also been drained."

Deputy Jones whistled. "Okay, who are we looking for?"

I gave the deputy a rundown of Carl Kieff's description. "He's staying at the inn. His stuff is still in the room, but no one's seen him today. He stood Clemmie up for coffee this morning."

"Should've known he was a crook," Clemmie grumbled from beside me in Aunt Thelma's apartment.

"The other guy is Jim … hang on. I took a picture of his driver's license."

"It's James Mahall. He goes by Jim," Clemmie answered before I could pull the photo up.

I relayed his full name and description to the deputy. "I'll text you over a copy of his driver's license. I'm not sure where he's staying at."

"The B & B," Clemmie answered once more.

"Did you hear that? He's staying with Shannon."

The deputy knew who I meant. "I'll put an APB out for these two men."

"And I'll drop the gift tag off here shortly."

I hung up with the deputy and looked for Clemmie. She'd wandered out of the living room. I found her down the hall in Aunt Thelma's small bedroom, her eyes flitting over the filled bookshelf. She ran her finger along the edges of the books and stopped suddenly, pulling out one to examine closely. Her face lit up with interest as she read the cover and leafed through the pages.

"What are you doing?" I asked, peering over her shoulder.

"What do you think I'm doing? I'm looking for a curse," Clemmie replied, not taking her eyes off the book. "Something that will make these men pay for hurting Thelma and taking my money."

I wanted to tell Clemmie that we couldn't go around cursing people, but I had to admit, I, too, wanted to see them pay. I was desperate to catch them and reverse Aunt Thelma's curse.

"Find anything good?" I asked, standing beside her.

"Not even close," Clemmie said, closing the book and placing it back on the shelf. "I feel so foolish for being so trusting with strangers online. And now I wonder if they were all working together."

"It's not your fault, Clemmie. Plenty of people meet their soulmates online and have great relationships," I reassured her, patting her back gently.

Clemmie chuckled at my about-face. "You were against it and now you're embracing it!"

"Not embracing it, exactly," but I smiled, nonetheless. It was a lighthearted moment on an otherwise heavy day.

Clemmie's mood sobered. "I know, but I should have been more careful. I should have seen the signs," she said, her voice filled with regret.

"We'll catch them, and we'll make them pay," I promised her. "But first, let's get the gift tag over to Deputy Jones."

Clemmie forced a half smile, nodding her head in agreement. "I think that's our best option for now," she said softly.

As we made our way out the door, I couldn't help but feel a gnawing sense of unease in my gut. This wasn't over yet, not by a long shot.

AS WE PULLED into the sheriff's department parking lot, we spotted Amber leading Jim up the steps toward the station's entrance. "Thought you were going to slip away, huh?" Amber taunted him. "Tried to give us the old slipperoo."

"What are you talking about? I was taking a nap," Jim looked bewildered.

"Sure, whatever you say," Amber replied sarcastically. "Get walkin'."

Clemmie was seething with anger, and I had to hold her back from confronting Jim right then and there. "Let me at him. Let. Me. At. Him." Clemmie's face was tight with anger, her hands fought to release her seat belt.

"Calm down. We need to let the sheriff do his job and gather evidence against him." If we weren't right in front of the sheriff's daughter, I don't think I'd been able to stop her.

"You might be right, but I don't like it." Clemmie took out her phone and placed a call.

"Now, who are you calling?"

"Connie. We need a truth potion, and we need one now."

I reached for Clemmie's phone. "You know that's not how this works." People had rights. You couldn't force potions down their throats without their consent.

"This is why Thelma needs to wake up. You are absolutely no fun."

"You know, I'm not even offended." Connie answered the phone. "False alarm," I told her. "But we might call back for a truth potion in a little bit."

"You know where to find me," Connie replied.

After hanging up, I handed Clemmie back her phone and said, "Come on, let's go."

The sheriff's department lobby was small and utilitarian, with linoleum floors, beige walls, and a reception desk manned by Dottie, a chatty midwestern woman who greeted visitors with a smile and a welcoming tone. A few chairs were scattered around the room, and a bulletin board hung on one wall, displaying community events. Behind the reception desk, a doorway led to the deputies' work area, which was separated from the public space by a metal counter. In the far corner of the room, a hallway led to the questioning rooms and a couple of jail cells, although they were out of sight from the lobby.

After saying hello to Dottie, Deputy Jones intercepted us.

"Here it is," I said, handing him the plastic baggie containing the gift tag.

He took it as evidence and then looked up at us with a raised eyebrow. "Do you two want to sit in on Jim's interview?"

"Are you kidding me?" I knew I was technically a deputy and all that, but I'd yet to sit in on an interview. I'd always been the one being interviewed.

"I thought you might want to hear what he has to say," he said, leading us down a hallway to a separate room.

"Any word on Carl?"

"Not yet. The sheriff and Amber are both out looking for him." Deputy Jones opened the door and ushered us inside. The observation room didn't have a two-way mirror like what you see in the movies. Instead, a large monitor was set up in front of us, displaying the footage from the camera in the interview room. We were each given a pair of headphones to listen in on the conversation.

The interview room itself was a plain-looking space with a small table and two chairs placed in the center. A camera was mounted on the wall above them, pointed towards the chairs. On the other monitor, we could see the back of Jim's head as he sat in one of the chairs while Deputy Jones sat in the other. It was a strange feeling, watching and listening in on an interrogation in real time, like we were a part of it but also completely removed from it.

Deputy Jones leaned forward, his eyes fixed on Jim. "Why don't we start from the top? What brings you to Silverlake?"

"I wanted to meet a friend," Jim replied, his voice trembling slightly.

"A friend? What's they're name?"

"Clemmie. Clemmie Braxton. I'm sure if you give her a call, she'll tell you who I am."

"Alright, and how did you meet Clemmie?"

"Online," Jim glanced up at the camera.

"Online?"

"Elder Mage Mingle," Jim mumbled, clearly embarrassed.

"You met her on an online dating website?"

"That's correct, sir."

Deputy Jones's eyes narrowed. "Have you ever been to Silverlake before?"

"No, sir."

"Do you know anyone else in town besides Clemmie?"

Jim shook his head. "No, sir. Just her. Well... I

did meet a few of her friends when we were out to dinner last night."

"Which friends?"

"I can't remember. It was Vince or Vance and his wife."

"What about Theo Crampton or Carl Kieff?" Deputy Jones asked.

Jim looked confused. "No, I don't know them. Should I?"

Deputy Jones continued to press him, trying to find any inconsistencies in his story. "Do you find it odd to surprise a woman you've never met before?"

Jim hesitated, then spoke up. "It's not traditional, I know. But I had to do something to catch her eye."

"Why?"

Jim seemed to struggle for the right words, but once he started talking, he couldn't seem to stop. "Clemmie's not like the other women I've met online. She's genuine, and smart, and independent too. She's not afraid to say what she thinks. I'm not sure how much experience you have with online dating." Deputy Jones admitted that it was not much, "Well, it's a whole toxic swamp. You have to wade through a lot of garbage. When you find someone special, you don't waste any time in letting them know."

"Letting them know what?"

"That you're serious. That you want to get to

know them more than over the computer. That you'd like a chance to have a meal together, face to face, and see if you click."

"And did you and Clemmie click?"

"I'd like to think so."

"But you don't know for sure?"

Jim shook his head.

"He's right, you know," Clemmie whispered, her eyes glued to the screen.

"What's that?" I asked, turning to her.

"He's right about me. I am smart and independent. I'm not afraid to speak my mind."

Jim continued, his voice wavering with emotion. "Clemmie's easy to talk to. We can talk about anything."

"I should have him write my next dating profile," Clemmie quipped, but even I could tell she was touched by his words.

"He's either truly a good man or a masterful liar," I said, trying to keep my voice low. I wondered if maybe Jim would be willing to drink a truth potion on his own. I was going to suggest it to Clemmie, but then again, was it worth pursuing a relationship with someone if you made them take a potion in order to trust them?

"Still, most men don't show up unannounced at someone's house. Especially when they live in…" Deputy Jones looked back at his notes, "Bucksnort, Tennessee."

Jim paused, then looked thoughtful before saying, "My wife used to say I was never romantic enough," he sighed. "I'm determined to do a better job with Clemmie. I haven't felt this way about anyone since Mary passed away."

"I've heard enough," Clemmie stood abruptly and took off her headphones.

"Wait, where are you going?" I stood too quickly with my headphones still on. The cord yanked me back down.

"He's clearly not our bad guy," Clemmie motioned to the monitor.

"We don't know that."

"Look at him. He's crying over his dead wife and saying all these sweet things about me. I take it back; I don't want to curse him anymore. It's Carl we have to go after." Clemmie turned around and walked right out the door.

"Clemmie, wait!" I took off the headphones and ran after her. She was already down the hall and approaching the front door with no signs of stopping. I waved a quick goodbye to Dottie, the fastest interaction I'd ever had with the receptionist, and followed Clemmie out.

Chapter 18

"Where are we going now?" I asked Clemmie once I caught up with her.

"To my shop. I'm calling an Enchanted Investigator's meeting."

"A what now?"

"It's what I've named our little mystery-solving group."

"Ah." For once, I was at a loss for words.

"We don't have much time if we want to find Carl and reverse your aunt's curse," Clemmie reminded me.

"You're right, we don't." I had texted Frederick a couple of times throughout the day, but there was still no change in Aunt Thelma's condition. He continued to promise he'd call me if things changed.

After we arrived at Village Square, I hung back for a minute to call Vance, insisting Clemmie go on without me. She had called Misty, Diane, and Roger on the way to see if they could join us at her tea shop. We needed to go over all the recent evidence and separate fact from fiction.

"Hey, how's it going?" Vance answered.

"Good. Do you have a minute?"

"A few. Court is on recess."

"Okay, well, we just sat in while Deputy Jones interviewed Jim."

"They found him quick."

"Yeah, I know. Still no word on Carl. Amber and the sheriff are still looking for him."

"How'd the interview go?"

"It was interesting. Clemmie wanted to curse him to the moon before he started talking."

"I can see that," Vance remarked.

"But Jim seems to genuinely be interested in her. I'm not sure what to make of it."

Vance paused for a moment before replying, "Interesting. I can look into him a bit more, see what I can find out."

"That would be great. I'll send you his driver's license picture." I pulled my phone away from my ear and sent Vance the photo.

"Got it. I'll get on it as soon as I can. It might be a couple of hours, but I'll try to squeeze it in when I can."

"Thanks, love."

"No problem. Let me know what else you need."

"Oh, I know. Can you see if there's a military connection between Theo, Carl, or Jim? I forgot to say something to Deputy Jones. Clemmie pulled me out of there before the interview was even over."

"On it."

We said our goodbyes, and I caught up with Clemmie at the tea shop. Misty, Diane, and Roger had already arrived and were seated around a table, sipping tea and nibbling on scones.

"Hey, guys," I said as I took a seat. "Any updates on Carl?"

Misty shook her head. "Nothing yet. I've been keeping an eye on the local news and social media, but so far, no leads."

Diane chimed in, "I did some research on that dating website. It's legit, but some people have said they were scammed."

"Scammed, how?" Misty asked.

"Credit card numbers hacked for their membership. Others confessed they were too trusting," Diane said as she refreshed her teacup.

"Don't any of you look at me. I already said I'm done with online dating," Clemmie announced.

No one said anything.

Finally, Roger spoke up. "I say we write down everything we know, and then we can start speculating what happened and who's to blame.

"That was my suggestion, too," I started to say when my cell phone started to buzz. I pulled out my phone and saw that it was from the bed and break-fast. I excused myself from the table and answered the call.

"Hello?" I said.

"Angelica? Hey, it's Shannon."

"Hey, Shannon, how's it going?" As the only two formal places to stay in Silverlake, well, other than the campground, it wasn't unusual for Shannon and me to call one another and check on room avail-ability.

"It's been better to tell you the truth."

"What's wrong?"

"You still working on your aunt's case?"

"Of course. Why?"

"I think I have some evidence for you. I called the sheriff's department, but Dottie told me everyone was busy. I didn't have time to stay on the line to wait. I'd already spent ten minutes I didn't have on the line with her."

"What did you find?"

"I'm not sure you heard, but Amber came and took that Jim Mahall in for questioning a while ago."

"I didn't realize he was staying with you, but I should have figured."

"He's been staying here the last few days, but here's the thing, Janet was cleaning his room, just normal housekeeping, and she found this note." Shannon paused for a moment before continuing, her voice low and serious. "It's a threat, telling him to leave town immediately or else. I know you're a deputy and all. Do you think you could pick it up? I don't want to leave it sitting here, and I'm the only one working at the moment."

"Absolutely. I'm on my way."

"Thank you so much."

I hung up the phone and turned to the group. "Sorry, guys. I have to go. Shannon found a threatening note in Jim's room."

"Oh no, I'm not having that," Clemmie replied, coming to Jim's defense.

"Jim's fine, I'm sure. I'll call Deputy Jones's direct line and fill him in."

"Do you want one of us to come with you?" Misty asked.

"No, you guys stay here and see what you can piece together. I'll be right back."

I quickly gathered my things and rushed out of the tea shop. As I made my way to the bed and breakfast, my mind raced with possibilities. Was this a genuine threat, or was someone trying to scare Jim away like they had tried with me? And if so, why?

The bed and breakfast sat on a quaint street corner, its charming exterior a mix of pale blue siding and white trim. A white picket fence ran around the property, with a gate leading to a small garden area filled with blooming flowers. Hanging baskets of petunias adorned the front porch, and a sign bearing the name "Lavender Inn" hung above the door. It was the type of place where you could imagine spending lazy afternoons reading a book on a porch swing or enjoying a cup of tea with friends.

As I approached the front door, Shannon peeked out and motioned me inside. "Thank goodness you're here. I found the note, but you're not going to believe this ... the message is gone!"

"Actually, I do believe it. The same thing happened to Vance and me yesterday."

"Are you serious?"

"Connie has a potion that can reveal the message." I wasn't sure how the spell worked. For example, did the message disappear after a certain amount of time or after someone read it? And how would it know the right person read it? Could it know?

I also thought of something else and quickly called Clemmie. "Can you text me a picture of Carl?"

"I already deleted the good-for-nothing scoundrels' photos from my phone, but hang on, I can pull them off line."

"Okay, thanks."

Shannon fetched the note while I was on the phone. She handed it over in a plastic baggie. I smiled at the packaging. "I wasn't sure what to put it in," Shannon explained.

"No, that's not why I'm laughing. I did something similar with another piece of evidence a little bit ago."

"Plastic bags are really quite useful," Shannon agreed.

My phone chimed, and I looked down at the message. Clemmie sent two pictures over. I turned my screen toward Shannon. "Does this guy look familiar to you?"

"I'd say so. I saw him this morning. He stopped in and asked about a room."

"He did? What time was that?"

"Oh, let me think … around ten o'clock? It was after the storm blew through. Why?"

"The sheriff wants to talk with him. Did he make a reservation or say anything in particular?"

"No, I gave him a tour of the place, and he said he'd get back with me. You don't think he wrote the note, do you?"

"I hate to say this, but I think it's a real possibility."

"He seemed like such a nice man. If he hadn't spent so much time admiring my garden, I probably wouldn't have remembered him."

"If you see him again, call me, or better yet, the sheriff right away. We're all looking for him."

"You got it. You stay safe, and let me know if there's anything else I can do. Your aunt is in my prayers."

"Thanks, Shannon."

Chapter 19

As I entered Connie's potion shop, the small bell attached to the door jingled, signaling my arrival. Connie looked up from behind her cauldron and greeted me with a smile. "Sorry, I'll be right with you. I need to pay attention to this for a minute."

"No problem."

Connie carefully measured out a handful of leaves and dropped them into a cauldron of boiling water. As she stirred the mixture, the steam turned a vibrant green color, and a strong scent of peppermint filled the room. She added a pinch of another unknown ingredient, which gave the brew a warm and comforting aroma. The liquid bubbled and hissed as Connie chanted a few words in a language I didn't recognize. She then added a dollop of an amber-colored liquid, stirring it in until it dissolved.

"Sorry, but if I don't add everything at just the right time, the whole potion will be ruined."

"No, that's okay. What is it?"

"It's a tummy tonic. It calms upset stomachs and aids in digestion." Connie ladled a sample of the potion into a glass bottle. The potion had a bright green color and a slightly thick consistency. It smelled strongly of peppermint with a hint of cinnamon and honey. Connie inspected the bottle and then took a sip. She bobbed her head side to side as if internally debating how it tasted. "It needs a little bit more honey," she said after a second.

I waited while Connie added another dollop of the amber-colored liquid to the cauldron and gave it a stir. "There, that should do it. Now, what can I do for you? Did you catch the bad guy yet?" she asked, wiping her hands on her apron.

I shook my head. "Not yet, but we have a lead. It turns out Clemmie's Boyfriend Number Two, Carl, is likely our man. We think he wiped out Clemmie's bank account and fled town after killing Boyfriend Number One, Theo."

Connie's eyebrows raised in surprise. "These are the guys she met online?"

"You got it."

"And what about Boyfriend Number Three?"

"That's Jim. Deputy Jones just interviewed him. He claims to be smitten with Clemmie and wants to sweep her off her feet. Vance is looking into him."

"Well, that's certainly a twist. Sheriff Reynolds and his deputies are on the lookout for Carl, I assume?"

"I doubted he was still in town even though his things were still at the inn, but Shannon said he stopped by the B & B this morning."

"That's weird. What did he do that for?"

"I think he was threatening Jim to get out of town." I took the blank piece of paper out of my purse. "Shannon said this had a threatening message on it, but it had disappeared before I got there. I was wondering if you still had that revealing potion anywhere around here?"

"Yeah, I have it. Let me grab it for you." Connie climbed up a ladder and retrieved a small bottle from a high shelf. Just like the first time, she pinched the bulb dropper, causing a few droplets of a shimmering blue liquid to fall onto the paper, creating a swirling pattern as they spread outward. As the potion soaked in, faint lines of inky black started to appear and gradually become more distinct. After a few moments, the threatening message was fully revealed. "Here you go," she said, handing me the paper. "It looks like you have some evidence to take to the sheriff."

I looked down at the paper, "You'll be next." The words were written in a bold, imposing script with calligraphic flourishes that gave the letters an air of authority. The style of the writing was the same as the first note.

I was just getting ready to leave Connie's potion shop when my phone buzzed. It was Percy on the line. "Hey, Jilly, that deputy friend of yours is here."

"Deputy Jones?"

"That's the one! He gave me a warrant for Carl's room. I told him, *Happy searching!* But I thought you'd want to know."

"You did good, Percy. Tell the deputy I'm on my way."

As I hung up the phone, Connie said to me, "Hey, before you go, see if Carl left his hairbrush behind. If we can get a strand of his hair, it might be enough of his essence to reverse Aunt Thelma's curse."

"Are you serious? I thought you needed … well, I guess I don't know what I thought, but I thought you needed the person."

"Nope. Anything that has residual traces of his essence, like hair or blood, will work. I could go on, but the list gets grislier."

I did not need Connie to paint a mental picture. I knew where her list was going. "No, I'm good. Let me run back there and see what I can find out." If I could've flown back to the inn, I would've.

❧

AS I ARRIVED at the inn, Deputy Jones's police cruiser was parked outside.

"They're thatta way," Percy pointed down the hall when I entered the lobby.

"Thanks, Percy. I owe you one." I found that it was always a good idea to reward a poltergeist when they made a mature call.

"Make it Rocky Road fudge from the Candy Cauldron, and we're even."

"You got it!" I jogged to Carl's room.

"Find anything good?" I asked, poking my head into the hotel room.

Deputy Jones had already begun to bag up Carl's belongings, which were spread throughout the room—clothes, books, a laptop, and other personal effects. He had a focused expression on his face as he worked quickly. Meanwhile, another deputy, Deputy Shreve, was searching the hotel room more carefully, looking under furniture and in drawers for anything else that might be useful in the investigation.

"Not yet," Deputy Jones held a book upside down to make sure there weren't any hidden notes inside.

"Did he leave his hairbrush, and if so, can I have it?"

Deputy Jones looked at me like I was nutty. "It's for Connie's reverse potion. She said she needs some of Carl's essence, or something like that, for it to work."

"Oh, in that case, let me see what we can do. I might need the hair for a DNA analysis down the road, but I'm sure we can spare a few strands."

For the first time since Aunt Thelma was cursed, I felt like the ending was in sight. A feeling of overwhelming relief washed over me, and I felt the weight of worry lifted from my shoulders. It was a glimmer of hope, a tiny spark of light in what had been a very dark situation.

"Oh, before I forget, Shannon found this note in Jim's room at the B & B. I took it to Connie. There's a hidden threat on it. Vance and I had a similar one yesterday, only Jim's is more menacing." I took the paper in its ziplock bag out of my purse and handed it over. "His said you'll be next."

"What did yours say?"

"I think back off, or something like that. Do you have any idea where Carl is?"

"No, but we found evidence that a large sum of money was transferred to his bank account, and a plane ticket to Mexico was purchased yesterday out of Atlanta airport. Multiple agencies are looking for him," the deputy replied, glancing back at Carl's suitcase.

As Deputy Jones spoke, Deputy Shreve interjected, "Hey, I found something in the bathroom. A large wad of cash. It was in his shaving case. A couple thousand at least."

Deputy Jones looked up in surprise. "I wonder where he got that money."

"It could be from Clemmie's account," I said.

Deputy Jones nodded thoughtfully. "True, but if that's where he got it from, why did he leave it behind?"

All three of us thought for a moment.

"You wouldn't leave cash behind if you could help it," Deputy Shreve said, counting out the dollar bills.

"True, but if he knew we were on to him, maybe he thought he better cut his losses and get out of town," I replied.

"That's probably more like it," Deputy Jones agreed. "Regardless, we need to make sure we have this bagged up properly and tagged for evidence."

Vance joined us at that time. "Hey, sorry I had to be in court."

"No, that's okay. I'm surprised you're already out," I remarked, leading Vance out of the room.

"So am I. The afternoon case took a last-minute plea bargain. Made everyone's life easier. So what's going on?"

I filled Vance in on the latest updates.

"Did you find any connection between Theo, Carl, and Jim?" I asked.

"Not really. Theo and Carl are both ex-military,

but different branches, and as far as I can tell, they never served together. Jim's story seems to check out. His wife passed away about five years ago. He doesn't have any priors, not even a parking ticket, and his credit is in great shape."

"I suppose that's a good thing."

"I wanted to do some more digging on Carl, see if we can help track him down, but I wanted to grab a quick bite to eat first. Do you want to get takeout and work at home for a bit?"

"Sure, but first, I need to get Carl's hairbrush to Connie." That comment required another explanation, but when I was finished, Vance and I had a plan.

<hr>

Chapter 20

<hr>

After dropping the hairbrush off to Connie, and her promising she'd call Charity and finish the counter-curse potion and call me when it was ready, we picked up Chinese takeout and headed home. Containers of sweet and sour chicken, beef and broccoli, vegetable fried rice, and egg rolls were spread out on the kitchen table as we settled in to eat.

For not the first time, I wished you didn't have to love someone in order to track them. I said as much to Vance in between bites of chicken. "Someone has to love the man, though, am I right?"

"Right, which is why I've been trying to contact Carl's family. His brother hung up on me. His parents are deceased, and his son hasn't called back yet."

"Any ex-wives?"

"Three, and none of them care if he's ever found again."

"Lovely." Rocky sat down like a boulder next to me, silently begging with his steadfast presence. I dropped a piece of broccoli for him. Rocky promptly woofed it down before deciding he didn't like broccoli and yacking it back up on the floor.

"Rocky, c'mon, man. We talked about this. Vegetables are good for you," Vance said while I stood up and got a napkin to clean it up. Rocky decided he was done begging and disappeared back to the couch for a nap.

Suddenly, Vance's phone rang. He looked at the caller ID and saw it was Max, Carl's son. "Hello, Max," Vance answered, putting it on speaker. "Thanks for calling back."

"Yeah, sure. The police just called me. What's going on?" Max asked, sounding worried.

"Long story short, we think your dad might be in some trouble. We need to find him. Do you have any idea where he could be?"

"He said he was meeting a friend in Silverlake, but that was it. I don't know anything else."

"Do you believe he could have done something to hurt someone or scam them?" Vance asked.

"What? No way! My dad can be a bit self-absorbed, especially when it comes to work, but he's a decent guy. He wouldn't kill or scam anyone. He's not like that."

Max came to his father's defense. It wouldn't do us any good to get him upset with us.

"Okay, okay, we believe you. We just need to find him to make sure he's safe," Vance said reassuringly. I replied with a look that suggested I thought otherwise. As far as I was concerned, Carl was guilty with a capital G. "Can you help us?" Vance ignored me and asked Max.

"I live a couple of hours away, but I'll leave now and head to Silverlake. I'll see what I can do."

"Hey, this is Anglica, Vance's wife. I'm also working to solve this case. Do you think you might be able to perform a tracking spell?" I said, joining in on the conversation.

"Sorry, no can do. No spells here. I'm a shifter, though, and I'll track him. Just you wait," Max replied.

"Alright then. When you get to Silverlake, come to Mystic Inn, and we'll get you set up with a room," I offered.

"Thanks, it'll be late, but I'll get to work right away," Max hung up, and Vance looked at me with a small smile.

"Looks like we might have a lead," he said, and I felt hope spark inside me once again.

With Max on the way and nothing else we could do, Vance and I settled in for a few hours of much-needed sleep. It was already two o'clock in the morning by the time Max made it to town. Percy called me as promised, but we decided we weren't going to do anything until sunrise.

The next morning, Vance and I stumbled into the inn. I was craving caffeine and something to eat. I grabbed a cup of coffee and a pastry and headed outside to the back patio. It was a beautiful day, and I wanted to enjoy it while I could.

As I sipped my coffee, I gazed out at the serene landscape. The Mystic Inn had a beautiful view of the lake. The sun was just starting to peek over the horizon, casting a golden glow over the scenery. It was a peaceful moment, and for a brief moment, I forgot about the chaos that had consumed my life for the past week.

But my peaceful moment was short lived as I spotted Maya, Theo's daughter, sitting out on the dock. She looked lost in thought, staring out over the calm waters. It was surprising to see her there since she was staying at the B & B. I debated whether to approach her, but something told me she could use a friend right then.

I went back inside and grabbed another cup of coffee, unsure how she took hers. I put a little cream and sugar in the cup and hoped for the best. As I approached her, I said, "Hi, Maya. Mind if I join you?"

She looked up at me with sad eyes and shook her head. "No, not at all."

I sat down next to her and handed her the

coffee. "I wasn't sure how you take it, so I added a little cream and sugar. I hope that's okay."

Maya gave me a small smile and took a sip. "Thanks, it's perfect. It's so peaceful here. I can see why my dad chose this inn."

I looked out over the lake with her. "Yes, it is beautiful. How are you holding up?"

Maya looked down at her coffee, and her eyes started to well up with tears. "I miss him so much. He was always there for me. He saw the best in others and would go out of his way to help anyone. He didn't deserve this."

I put a hand on her shoulder in comfort. "I promise we'll get justice for your dad. We won't stop until we do."

Maya nodded and wiped away a tear. "Thank you. It means a lot to me." Maya took a shaky breath. "I'm not even sure what to do right now. Being here, right here, makes me feel closer to my dad, but I know I can't stay here forever."

"You can stay here for as long as you like. Take all the time you need."

"Thanks, Angelica."

I left Maya and headed back toward the inn's back deck, ready to meet back up with Vance and see if Max was up yet. I knew he only had a couple hours of sleep, but he sounded just as eager to find his dad as we were. Connie said the potion was almost complete. It just needed to simmer for two hours, and then we'd meet up at the hospital to see if it worked.

I saw Vance through the inn's sliding glass door and headed in his direction until something on the Enchanted Trail caught my attention. Enchanted Trail was a beloved outdoor path that circled the lake, providing a serene and picturesque route for locals and visitors alike. The trail was lined with tall trees, their branches reaching out to create a canopy overhead, and the ground was covered in wood chips. The trail meandered through the peaceful surroundings, offering glimpses of the shimmering lake through the foliage.

Paths branched off from Enchanted Trail, leading to different parts of the town. One led to Village Square, the bustling business district where shops and restaurants thrived. Another path led to the nearby campground, a popular spot for outdoor enthusiasts. The trail itself was frequented by walkers, joggers, and nature enthusiasts who enjoyed the tranquil atmosphere and the beauty of the surrounding landscape. And right now, a beautiful red fox was working the trail, sniffing his way down the narrow path.

As I observed the red fox, it moved with a purpose, its nose constantly close to the ground. It reminded me of the focused determination of a police dog in search of a missing person or contraband. The fox meticulously examined the trail, occasionally pausing to investigate a particular spot more closely. He moved in a zigzag pattern, leaving no stone unturned as if he knew exactly what he was searching for.

A thought crossed my mind. Max had mentioned that he was a shifter, capable of transforming into an animal of his choosing. Could this be Max in his fox form, using his keen senses to track down his father?

The more I watched the fox, the more I became convinced it was Max. Except whatever trail he was tracking seemed to go cold about fifty yards down the trail. There was a moment of hesitation in his movements. He sniffed the air, his ears perked up as if straining to catch a particular scent. His confusion became evident as he started to backtrack, retracing his steps on the Enchanted Trail.

The fox's confident stride turned into a cautious trot, and its nose was no longer focused on the ground. As I watched Max work, I felt empathetic to his setback. I understood the frustration that came with pursuing a trail that suddenly went cold.

As the fox drew near, I extended my hand, offering a gesture of connection. "Max, I presume?"

The fox nodded. "I'm Angelica. I'll let you shift back, and then we can meet up in the lobby. Sound good?" I offered.

The fox nodded, and I left him to do his thing. I could shift, but I was a witch at heart. Because of my magic, I could pull clothes into my shift. Not everyone was as lucky. Talk about an awkward way to meet someone.

❧

MAX MET us in the cozy lobby of the Mystic Inn, his sandy blond hair tousled from shifting and his striking blue eyes filled with determination.

"Hi, I'm Angelica. This is my husband, Vance," I said, formally introducing ourselves. Percy glared at Max as if he was personally responsible for cursing Aunt Thelma.

"Max Kieff," the man said, shaking our hands in turn.

"Here, let's move this conversation to my office," I motioned for Max to follow us. The office would ensure our conversation remained private, away from prying ears. Once inside, I closed the door behind us, creating a shield of privacy.

Max leaned against the edge of my desk, his presence emanating both strength and vulnerability. He spoke with a quiet resolve, "I can smell my father's scent, I followed it on the trail, but it suddenly goes cold after the first bend. It's as if he vanished."

I furrowed my brow, deep in thought. "Could your father have somehow cloaked his scent? Concealed it through magic or some other means?"

Max shook his head, his voice tinged with uncertainty. "Not that I'm aware of. Shifting is a part of our nature, but magic is a different realm altogether. I don't think his abilities extend that far. I know mine don't."

I twisted my lips in thought. If Carl was working with a witch, they could cover his tracks. "Wait a second, why didn't I think of this sooner?"

"What?" Vance and Max said at the same time.

"Carl couldn't have written the notes. They have a spell on them, remember?" I said to Vance.

"Does that mean he's innocent?" Max looked hopeful.

"Or that he's working with someone," Vance said what I didn't want to.

Max started to protest. I understood that he wanted to defend his dad, but I always wanted him to look at the facts. I said as much to Max. "Regardless, we need to find your dad."

"The police said he bought a ticket to Mexico," Vance said.

"And that flight was this morning. He wasn't on it," Max answered.

"No one saw him leave town. All of his belongings are still here," I continued.

"So where is he?" Vance asked.

None of us had an answer to that.

"There's no other scent trail?" I asked Max.

"Not as fresh," Max replied.

I twisted my lips in thought.

"I think I have an idea," I said, my voice filled with cautious optimism. "We know witches can use magic to cloak a scent," I motioned between me and Vance, "but can we use it to uncloak it as well? If so, we might be able to trace Carl's scent back to its source."

Max looked at me with a mixture of hope and curiosity. "Is that even possible?"

I nodded, a determined gleam in my eyes. "Magic has a way of balancing itself out. If someone has used magic to conceal Carl's scent, there might be a way to reverse it. And I know just the witch to ask."

Max's eyes widened with interest. "Who?" Vance raised his eyebrows, mirroring the question.

"Connie," I replied confidently. "She's one of the smartest witches I know, next to Aunt Thelma. She has a wealth of knowledge when it comes to charms and enchantments. If there's a way to uncloak a scent, she might have the answer." Connie was a licensed potion master, but her knowledge went way beyond bubbling brew.

Vance chimed in. "It's worth a try. We've exhausted all other leads, and this might just be our breakthrough."

I reached for my phone and dialed Connie's number, my fingers tapping nervously against the device. After a few rings, she answered, her voice filled with warmth and curiosity. "It's almost done, promise," Connie said when our lines connected.

"Oh no, it's not that. I know you're busy with Aunt Thelma's potion, but I have a quick question. Is there such a thing as an uncloaking charm? We think someone used magic to cloak Carl's scent, and we're wondering if there's a way to reverse it."

There was a moment of silence on the other end, and then Connie's voice returned, filled with intrigue. "An uncloaking charm? Now that's an interesting concept. I don't recall encountering such a specific charm, but Charity might know."

"Really?"

"Long story, but she had an ex-boyfriend who was fond of cloaking spells. She put an end to that and the relationship after tracking him one night. I don't know how she did it, but I'm sure she'll tell you."

"Okay, awesome. I'll give Charity a call."

Chapter 21

"An uncloaking charm is not something that can be easily found in spellbooks," Charity began, her voice thoughtful. She was kind enough to meet our group at the inn. "But here's what I did." She reached into her bag and pulled out a small leather-bound notebook, flipping through the pages until she found a section labeled *Uncover the Truth*. Charity read through the notes to refresh her memory.

"Okay, so what you need to do is create a unique scent signature that counteracts the cloaking spell," Charity's finger traced the words on the page. "By infusing an item with a distinct aroma that resonates with Carl's essence, you should be able to reveal his hidden scent trail."

She looked at us as if all of her words made perfect sense.

"Um, say what now?" I looked around the

room. Vance and Max had similar clueless expressions.

Charity pressed on, reading from her grimoire. "It requires a combination of magical herbs, essence extraction, and precise spellcasting, but the resulting scent would act as a beacon, guiding you to the source and uncloaking the concealed trail."

Vance leaned forward. "Wait, how do we go about infusing an item with this scent signature?"

"And what essence extraction?" I added. It didn't sound like a pleasant process.

Charity smiled warmly. "It's not as complicated as it sounds. You'll need something that Carl frequently used or carried with him. It could be a personal item, like a piece of clothing, a favorite accessory, or even his shaving kit. By imbuing it with the unique scent concoction, we can tap into the magical resonance and create a trail that bypasses the cloaking spell."

"So, if we can find one of his personal belongings, we can use this uncloaking charm to track him?" Max clarified.

Charity nodded. "Yes. Once we have the infused item, we'll need to perform a ritual near the starting point of the trail, connecting our intention to unravel the enchantment. It should guide us to his location."

I nodded, understanding the general gist of it. "The only problem is, Deputy Jones already searched the room. He bagged and tagged all of Carl's belongings."

"Do you think he'll let us use something?" Max asked.

"I guess there's only one way to find out," I replied.

"YOU WANT TO DO WHAT NOW?" Deputy Jones replied after I explained our plan. We'd driven directly to the sheriff's department in hopes it would be harder to turn down our request in person. Charity ran to get the rest of the spell's ingredients and then was going to meet us back at the trailhead.

I repeated my request, feeling a mix of urgency and determination. "We need one of Carl's personal belongings to use in a scent-infusion ritual. It could help us track him down."

"That's a new one. I haven't heard of this spell, but it could be useful for the station. What exactly do you plan to do with this item?" Deputy Jones eyed the sheriff's office door. I knew what he was thinking: *How much trouble would I get in if they destroyed evidence?*

"To be honest, I don't fully understand the spell. Charity's explanation was above me, but I don't think the item will be damaged. Let me double-check." I gave Charity a quick call. Charity confirmed that the item wouldn't be ruined. "I was right. We just need the item for the spell and then you can have it back."

"Alright then. If it helps find Carl, I'm willing to lend you one of his personal belongings."

Max's eyes brightened. "Do you have his watch? It's a sentimental item, a gift from my grandfather. He wouldn't have left that behind willingly."

Deputy Jones nodded. "Yeah, we do have his watch. It's in the evidence locker. Let me grab it for you."

As Deputy Jones left the room, Max turned to me and Vance. "Thank you for working so hard to find my dad. It means the world to me."

"Mm-hmm, sure." I smiled on the outside, but on the inside, I still wasn't convinced Carl wasn't our bad guy. But I was convinced that finding him would bring us one step closer to the truth.

A few minutes later, Deputy Jones returned with Carl's watch, carefully placing it in a small evidence bag. He handed it to Max, who held it gently as if it were a precious artifact.

Deputy Jones nodded. "Let me know after you work the spell and if you need backup. I'm waiting for a call from the Agency of Paranormal Particularities." The agency rounded up bad supernaturals all around the world. It sounded like they'd been called in to find Carl. Deputy Jones looked down at his phone as if willing it to ring.

"I'll give you a call as soon as I know something," I promised, and together, Max, Vance, and I left the station and headed back to the inn.

WE REACHED a clearing near the trailhead, surrounded by towering trees that cast long shadows on the ground. Charity had arrived ahead of us, her bag of magical ingredients at the ready.

"Connie said the potion is ready. Is it okay if she gives it to your aunt, or do you still want to wait until you can be there?" Charity asked.

I didn't even hesitate. "Give it to her, it's okay."

"Are you sure?" Vance questioned me.

"Absolutely. I thought I wanted to be there, and I do, but this is more important. I don't want to make Aunt Thelma wait any longer to wake up."

"Okay, I'll text Connie." Charity took out her phone and did just that.

Under the high sun, its rays beaming down with relentless intensity, we embarked on our journey down the Enchanted Trail. The summer air hung heavy with humidity, wrapping around us like a warm embrace. The trail was flanked by towering pine trees, their scent mingled with the earthy fragrance of the forest floor. As we walked, our footsteps echoing softly on the woodland path, the interplay of sunlight and shade created a dappled pattern on the ground.

"Here's where I lost the scent." Max held his father's watch tightly in his hand, his fingers tracing the familiar contours of the timepiece.

"All right, everyone," Charity's voice filled with confidence. "Let's get to work. Gather around and form a circle. Focus your thoughts on Carl and the need to uncover his hidden trail."

We formed a tight circle on the narrow path. Vance and I held our wands at the ready. Vance stood on one side of Max while I stood on the other. The sun cast a warm golden glow over our faces as we closed our eyes and centered our thoughts.

Charity stepped forward, her voice steady as she began to chant incantations, calling upon the forces of nature and magic. I cracked open my eye and saw blue-green energy swirling around her as the magic continued to build.

As Charity reached the climax of the spell, she motioned for Max to step forward. He placed his father's watch on the ground, right at the center of our circle, while Charity continued to chant the incantation.

Max took a deep breath, his face a mask of determination. He closed his eyes and focused his shifting abilities, channeling the essence of the fox within him. As Max shifted, there was a crackling sound of electricity that filled the air, followed by a low hum as his body completed its transformation. Max was now a beautiful red fox. His fur shimmered in the sunlight, glimmering like copper in the sun.

The magic continued to build. A surge of energy filled the air, crackling with a mix of anticipation and hope. The watch pulsed with a soft light as if responding to the spell's magic. A soft hum, almost like a whisper, accompanied the light.

Suddenly, the air shifted, and a faint trail of Carl's scent began to emanate from the watch. Blue whisps spiraled and danced in the air, weaving its way through the forest, leading us deeper down the trail.

Max's eyes gleamed with determination as he followed the scent, his swift fox paws gracefully navigating the terrain. We followed closely behind, our wands at the ready, guided by the enchanting aroma that had been unleashed.

The trail seemed to come alive with otherworldly energy, branches whispering secrets and leaves rustling in anticipation. The trail led us through a series of winding paths, up from the lakebed, as if Carl's scent was leaving breadcrumbs for us to follow.

As we continued our pursuit, Max suddenly halted, his fox form standing tall and alert. He looked back at us, his eyes shining with excitement and a sense of purpose. Without hesitation, he dashed forward, his swift strides carrying him down the trail.

"Wait!" Vance shouted, but Max didn't slow down. I hadn't expected him to. We followed the best we could, hearts pounding with a mixture of hope and trepidation.

The spell had worked.

We were on the right track, and with each passing moment, we drew closer to uncovering the truth and finding Carl.

As we ventured deeper down the path, the echoes of our footsteps mingled with the sound of wildlife and the rustling of leaves. Our path was illuminated by glimpses of the sun breaking through the tree canopy, but our surroundings grew darker as we went deeper into the woods, eventually losing sight of Max altogether, his agile form disappearing into the foliage ahead.

I hadn't run regularly for over a year now, and I was struggling to keep up. Charity had given up half a mile or so back, but I pressed on, my lungs burning and side aching. Vance continued on, his shoes rhythmically thundering down the trail.

"Where'd he go?" I said, catching up to Vance where the trail split.

He put his hands on his hips, catching his breath. "I don't know." The worry in his eyes mirrored the unease that settled in my chest.

I looked down the left and then the right for any

sign of direction, like tracks to follow.

Before we could make up our minds, a haunting howl pierced the air. It was a cry of pain and urgency, echoing through the stillness of the forest.

"This way!" The sound jolted us into action, and we sprinted toward the source.

Pushing through the undergrowth and breaking through the final barrier of trees, we found ourselves at the back of the campground. It had to be. If not, I wasn't sure where we were. Old cabins stood before us, weathered and forgotten.

Vance touched his forefinger to his lips in a shhh motion. He didn't have to worry; I wasn't about to say anything as I struggled to control my breathing and racing heart.

We approached one of the dilapidated structures with caution, aware of the danger that lurked within.

Peering through a cracked window, Vance and I gasped in unison. We stood rooted to the spot, our eyes glued to the spectacle that was before us. Carl had been bound and gagged, sitting in a weathered chair. His clothes were ripped and disheveled from a struggle.

"Is that ... Carl?" Vance muttered, his voice barely holding back the shock.

I couldn't find any words to respond. All I could do was nod my head, my hand instinctively rising to cover my mouth.

"Is he alive?" Vance asked.

I took a closer look. It was hard to tell. He wasn't moving. "I don't know."

As we assessed the situation, our attention was momentarily diverted by a sudden whimper coming from above us. Looking up, our eyes widened in disbelief. Max, hanging upside down by his tail. He seemed to be caught in a booby trap triggered by his unintended movements.

"Max! Oh my gosh," I looked at my husband, "Who should we rescue first?"

"Let's get Max down in case he's in pain."

"Okay, right."

Just as we were about to fully focus on rescuing Max, a chilling voice cut through the air, sending shivers down our spines. "Guys, look out!" Charity called out. "She's going to curse you."

I whipped around behind me, ready to defend myself. It was Maya, standing before us with a malevolent smirk, her wand extended and ready for action. In her grasp was Charity, her hair held tightly as she was forced forward like a hostage.

My heart pounded in my chest as I looked to Vance, our gazes locked in silent communication. The urgency of the situation was palpable, and the question hung in the air between us—how are we going to get out of this?

Time seemed to slow as our attention shifted back to Maya, her malevolent intentions clear. We tightened our grips on our wands, ready to defend ourselves and those we cared about. The determination in our eyes mirrored the steely resolve in Maya's.

Maya's face contorted with anger and desperation. "How many people do I have to curse around here?!" Her voice cracked with frustration, revealing the unraveling state of her mind. "I was just trying to protect my father!"

Vance and I exchanged a brief glance, a mixture of concern and curiosity etched on our faces. We cautiously approached, keeping a safe distance, our wands still at the ready. "Maya, what are you talking about?" Vance asked, his voice laced with both caution and empathy.

A bitter laugh escaped Maya's lips as tears streamed down her face. "My father, Theo, was being taken advantage of by women he met online. I couldn't stand seeing him hurt and used anymore." Her voice quivered with a mix of anger and sadness. "When I found out he was planning to meet Clemmie, I decided to intervene. I wanted to scare her away, to make her see that these online relationships were dangerous."

Her words hung heavy in the air as the weight of her actions slowly became clear. Maya took a shuddering breath, her voice filled with remorse. "I... I cursed the necklace, hoping it would convince

Clemmie to stay away. But then, things went horribly wrong."

Vance's brows furrowed as he pieced the case together.

"What happened, Maya?" I kept my voice gentle.

Maya's voice trembled as she continued her confession. "When my father discovered what I had done, we had a terrible fight. He was furious and frightened, and in the midst of it all, he lost his balance and fell. He hit his head on the nightstand … and he … he didn't survive." Her words trailed off, lost in a sea of regret.

A wave of sympathy washed over me as I listened to Maya's heartbreaking revelation. The pain in her voice was palpable, her guilt consuming her. "Maya," I spoke softly, my voice filled with compassion. "You thought you were protecting your father, but these actions... They weren't the answer."

Maya's tear-filled eyes met mine, her grip on Charity loosening slightly. "I know," she whispered, her voice heavy with remorse. "I realized that too late. And in my desperation, I concocted a plan to frame one of Clemmie's online boyfriends, hoping it would be the perfect cover-up." She took a deep breath, her voice wavering. "I opened a fake bank account in Clemmie's name, transferred the money, and then withdrew it, making it look like one of the boyfriends had stolen it."

The weight of Maya's confession hung heavy in the air, the truth of her actions laid bare. Vance and I exchanged a somber glance, a shared understanding of the tangled web of deception that had brought us to this moment.

But there was no time to dwell on the past. Maya's grip tightened once again on Charity's hair, a flicker of desperation in her eyes. Her wand was extended, poised to strike. "Don't come any closer! I won't let you ruin everything!" she shouted, a mix of fear and defiance in her voice.

Our wands remained steady in our hands, ready to defend ourselves if necessary. But deep down, amidst the chaos and confusion, I couldn't help but feel a flicker of empathy for Maya. She was a young woman who had lost her way, consumed by fear and misguided intentions.

I watched Maya's eyes dart around, her mind seemingly in a whirlwind of desperation and determination. She muttered to herself, her voice shaky yet resolute. "I have to do this. I'll erase their memories … kill those two … then it will all be fine. I'm still in control."

My heart raced as I realized the gravity of Maya's plan. Lives were at stake, and I couldn't let her carry out such a tragic act. With each passing moment, the urgency grew, and I knew I had to act swiftly.

Maya got off one warning shot, a freezing

charm that went wide before we sprang into action.

Determined to prevent Maya's destructive plan from unfolding, we moved with swift coordination. Vance conjured a shield, deflecting Maya's freezing charm, while Charity countered with a stunning spell that momentarily staggered Maya.

I seized the opportunity, channeling my magic through my wand and directing it toward Maya. "Potentia exuo!" I shouted, unleashing a powerful disarming charm. Maya's wand flew out of her hand, clattering onto the ground.

Realizing her control was slipping away, Maya's eyes widened in a mixture of fear, anger, and desperation. She lunged forward, attempting to regain her wand and continue her desperate fight.

Vance shouted a magical incantation as he weaved a web of binding spells around Maya, confining her movement in a single spot. "Charity!" he commanded, and she followed his lead with a stunning spell that sapped away at Maya's defenses and further diminished her ability to resist. I joined in, casting a suppression charm to subdue Maya's magical powers, ensuring that she could no longer wield her spells against us. "It's done," I said, catching my breath. We had finally rendered Maya powerless.

With Maya safely restrained, our attention quickly turned to Max and Carl, both in need of rescue. Working in harmony, we swiftly moved to untangle Max from the rope that held him captive. Vance carefully maneuvered around the branches, untwisting the knots with precision as I provided support from below. Moments later, Max was free, and he ran off once more to shift back and redress. I knew he'd rejoin us momentarily.

Vance and I then moved on to free Carl while Charity kept an eye on Maya, calling the sheriff in the process.

The cabin's door creaked open, revealing the sight of Carl bound and gagged. I could see a glimmer of hope flickering in his eyes. We wasted no time in removing the restraints, our touch gentle yet purposeful, freeing him from the confines of his captivity.

As Carl took a deep breath, regaining his voice, he uttered words of gratitude. "I can't thank you enough. You've saved me. I don't even know who that woman was and what this was all about."

"Her name is Maya Crampton, and she framed you for her father's murder," Vance said.

"He was also dating Clemmie," I supplied.

"We can go into more detail later, but right now, let's get you to the hospital." Carl stood on shaky legs, and we led him out of the cabin.

As the sound of approaching sirens grew louder, signaling the arrival of the authorities, we would ensure that Carl's name was cleared and that truth would prevail.

Epilogue

In the moments that followed, the pieces of the puzzle fell into place. Maya was apprehended by the authorities and brought to justice for her crimes. The truth behind Carl's situation was uncovered, and he was cleared of any wrongdoing. The community breathed a collective sigh of relief, grateful that the darkness that had plagued their small town had been vanquished.

With Maya behind bars, the focus shifted to Aunt Thelma and the counter-curse potion. Connie, armed with the right culprit, worked tirelessly to perfect the potion. Minutes turned into hours, but finally, the moment arrived when she presented us with the final concoction.

Gathered in Aunt Thelma's hospital room, Frederick, Vance, and I stood anxiously as Connie carefully administered the counter-curse potion. The room was filled with a mixture of hope and apprehension, the weight of the moment hanging in the air. We exchanged nervous glances, our hearts pounding with anticipation.

Frederick, his hand tightly clasping Aunt Thelma's, whispered words of encouragement. "You've got this, Thelma. We're all here for you." His voice carried a blend of determination and love, reflecting the unwavering support he had for Aunt Thelma.

Vance reached out to squeeze my hand, his eyes filled with a mix of hope and relief. "She's strong, Angelica. She'll overcome this curse. I just know it." His words were a comforting reminder that we were in this together, bound by our shared love for Aunt Thelma.

With bated breath, we watched as Connie gently tilted the vial, allowing the potion to touch Aunt Thelma's lips. Time seemed to slow down, each second stretching into an eternity as we waited for a sign, any sign, that the potion was taking effect.

And then, like a flicker of life rekindled, Aunt Thelma's eyes fluttered open. The room was filled with a collective gasp of relief and joy. A radiant smile spread across Aunt Thelma's face, illuminating the room with its warmth and happiness.

Tears welled up in my eyes as I leaned in closer, unable to contain my emotions. "Aunt Thelma, you're awake!" I exclaimed, my voice filled with a mix of awe and gratitude. "We've missed you so much."

Aunt Thelma's voice was soft and filled with a profound sense of love as she whispered, "I could hear you all, you know. Your kind words, your well wishes. I love you all in so many different ways." Her words washed over us, filling our hearts with a sense of profound connection and appreciation.

Frederick squeezed Aunt Thelma's hand tighter, his voice filled with affection. "I love you too, Thelma. You're the light of my life."

Aunt Thelma's gaze swept across the room, landing on each of us with a deep sense of love and gratitude. "You're all my family. I am so blessed to have you by my side."

Tears welled up in our eyes as Aunt Thelma's words washed over us. It was a profound moment, a reminder of the strength of familial bonds and the enduring power of love. We had come together, faced adversity head-on, and emerged stronger than ever.

In the days and weeks that followed, life slowly returned to normal in our small lakeside community. We shared meals, laughter, and stories, cherishing the moments we had together. Aunt Thelma's recovery was swift, her spirit vibrant as ever. She became a beacon of light, a symbol of resilience and perseverance.

As for Vance and me, our bond deepened

through the trials we had faced together. We found solace in each other's arms, knowing that no matter what challenges lay ahead, we had each other's unwavering support.

~

DEAR READER,

Thank you for joining me on this incredible journey in Silverlake. I hope you enjoyed immersing yourself in the world I've created and getting to know the characters that have become dear to my heart.

If you'd like to stay connected and be the first to know about exciting updates, exclusive content, and upcoming releases, I invite you to sign up for my author newsletter. By subscribing, you'll gain access to behind-the-scenes insights, sneak peeks, and special promotions just for my loyal readers.

Sign up here: https://stephaniedamore.com/newsletter/

I value your support and look forward to sharing more stories and adventures with you. Your enthusiasm and feedback mean the world to me, and I'm grateful to have you as part of my reader community.

xoxo,

Stephanie

**What do you think?
Should I write more Mystic Inn Mysteries?
Email me and tell me:
steph.damore@gmail.com**

Stephanie Damore Complete Works

MYSTIC INN MYSTERIES
Witchy Reservations
Eerie Check In
Spooked Solid
Untimely Departure
Midnight at Mystic Inn
Bewitch Break Inn
Potions, Poison, and Pumpkin Spice
Jingle Bells and Wedding Spells
Spellbinding Secrets
Fatal Enchantment

SPIRITED SWEETS MYSTERIES
Bittersweet Betrayal
Decadent Demise

Red Velvet Revenge
Sugared Suspect

WITCH IN TIME
Better Witch Next Time
Play for Time
Time Will Tell

BEAUTY SECRETS SERIES
Makeup & Murder
Kiss & Makeup
Eyeliner & Alibis
Pedicures & Prejudice
Beauty & Bloodshed
Charm & Deception

A DROP DEAD *Famous Cozy Mystery*
Mourning After

About the Author

Stephanie Damore is a USA Today bestselling author known for her captivating cozy mysteries featuring smart and sassy sleuths. With a passion for weaving magic and romance into her stories, Damore's books are perfect for readers who crave a delightful mix of happily ever after and whodunit.

For information on new releases and fun giveaways, visit her Facebook group: Paranormal Mystery Coven

www.facebook.com/groups/
paranormalcozymystery/

 twitter.com/stephdamore

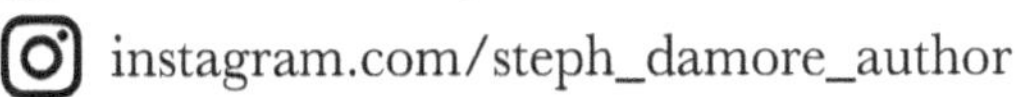 instagram.com/steph_damore_author

 bookbub.com/profile/stephanie-damore